DEMONS OF BATHORIA

BYRON THE BARBARIAN
BOOK THREE

JEFF O'BRIEN

ISBN-13: 978-1544686127

ISBN-10: 1544686129

DEDICATION

For Craig Mullins,
My brother in barbarians, aliens, bigfeet, metal, and other awesome stuff.

CONTENTS

ACKNOWLEDGMENTS

It should be acknowledged by everyone that barbarian fiction is in desperate need of a comeback. It can happen.

ONE

The once bright stone walls and granite pillars of the throne room were covered in soot and ash, nasty byproducts of the sudden goblin invasion. Like a plague, the vile monsters poured in through the open windows, filling the room with their stench and clouding the air with filth.

Two buxom sword-wielding twins and their mentor had been in the middle of a late night training session, and were now all that stood against the heinous creatures.

Mardra mustered up a smile as her broadsword split the head of a pig-faced goblin, and rather than wince, she curled her lips into a snarl of determination as black, gooey blood and bits of brain splatted against her comely, angelic face.

In opposite corners of the room her protégés were holding their own with near-equal finesse and cunning. Mardra tried not to lose focus on her own survival as she watched on proudly while Leigh and Lynette sliced down goblin after goblin with barely a show of effort. Her tutelage had not been in vain. The lovely twins, sent to her by her lost love Byron, were fast learners. But with the thought of Byron came another, deeper distraction. Mardra snapped back to the present as a goblin blade whizzed past her ear, nearly taking a piece of it off. A rapid-fire elbow to the snotty snout of the goblin knocked it back a few steps, and a quick upward jab of her sword skewered the jaw and skull of her attacker. Another one down. Dozens more to go.

This battle was the first moment of fun Mardra had had since she took the crown and became queen and ruler of the territory, aside from her occasional spontaneous bedtime romps with Leigh and Lynette. The twins had learned far more than combat from the energetic queen. But as far as governmental matters were concerned, Mardra had grown bored on her throne, regretting her decision. Or was it the absence of the man who had refused her offer of kingship that made the throne a dull place to sit? And were sexual escapades with the twins merely her way of making up for Byron's absence? Mardra felt no jealousy over Byron fucking the twins before sending them her way, but if he had them, then she had to have them too. In a strange way it made her feel closer to her missing lover.

"Mardra! Look out!"

Lynette's warning again snapped Mardra from a daydream of Byron, and saved her from losing her left arm. A duo of goblins had cornered her in her loss of focus, and for perhaps the first time ever in her storied career of combat she found herself at a disadvantage.

"Lovely set a' tits on ya'!" growled the goblin to her right, spittle and black gunk dripping from its mouth. "I think I'll have me-self a bit a' fun before I kill ya'!"

"Save some for me, will ya, Glokar," growled the equally repulsive monster to Mardra's left. "Don't be stingy now. We can take turns on 'er!"

Mardra had learned early on in life that a good set of tits could be used to one's advantage in many ways. That was why she dropped her sword and allowed Glokar to reach beneath the fabric of her skimpy training garb and cop a good feel of her bosom. All too easily she snatched away his sword and plunged it through his distracted face, twisting it to the left and pushing it farther down and into the other goblin's chest, making a kebob of their twitching bodies before pulling it out in a spray of black blood.

The reluctant queen had now reached the point in battle where she found herself impatient to see the end. From the beginning of the sudden goblin onslaught she had been pacing herself, as had Leigh and Lynette, keeping most of their energy on reserve for this very moment. With her free hand she retrieved her sword from the floor and spun into a rapid ballet of slices and swings, taking off heads and limbs in a double-whirlwind of spinning blades. The twins had seen her sudden blast of action and followed along, quickly reducing the number of attackers and cluttering the throne room floor with heaps of hideous corpses.

"Bring it in, girls!" Mardra shouted. Upon hearing her command Leigh and Lynette made quick work of their closest combatants and ran to Mardra. The three stood back to back to back, letting the remaining two-dozen or so goblins encircle them. "Their numbers are low enough now that we can let them bring the fight to us. And good work, girls. I see not a scratch on either of you."

"You've taught us well, Mardra," said Leigh.

"Byron hadn't lied when he said you would do so," added Lynette.

Fuck. Byron. Mardra hadn't wanted to hear that name brought up. Only one way to block it out for the time being.

"Attack!" she bellowed.

The trio burst into a rapid routine of choreographed kicks, elbows and sword thrusts that Mardra had taught the twins. Quickly the mindless goblins fell. All muscle and little brain made them weak opponents against such a well thought out and rehearsed onslaught. Within moments the women were the only three living creatures in the throne room. It seemed all too easy.

"Now what?" asked Leigh.

Mardra lowered her sword and took a seat on the altar where her throne lay toppled on its side. "We take a breather, then go about figuring out what the fuck just happened."

"Sounds good," said Lynette, and the twins took a seat on either side of Mardra.

"You've been cut, Lynette," said Mardra, pointing to a splotch of red blood on the girl's short dress.

"Barely a scratch," scoffed Lynette. "And it was from my own sword. I haven't yet mastered all the twirls in that last routine we did."

"Fair enough," said Mardra. "But you still lose to Leigh."

Leigh let out a refreshing laugh. "Even now that we're past training and fighting for our lives, you still insist on stirring up a little sibling rivalry."

"A good trainer knows her apprentices' weaknesses," said Mardra. "A little innocent competition keeps a warrior on her toes."

"I'm more alert due to the fact that one moment we were practicing with our swords, and the next thing we know an army of goblins sneaks in through the windows and tries to kill us," reasoned Lynette. "I'm just wondering how they managed to pull that off without alerting anyone in or around the castle."

"Seems to me that some dark magic is afoot, or the rest of the castle was indeed alerted," said Mardra. "And I can't imagine this siege is over. And who or whatever sent this ambush our way is surely trying to send us a message as well, and has more in store for us."

Suddenly the doors of the throne room burst open and in came a blinding light. The women squinted and covered their eyes, but rose to their feet and brandished their swords, ready for anything. When the light died down they saw framed in the doorway an old, scraggly-bearded man with one eye of solid white. Accompanying him was a young, nearly nude woman of impressive beauty, clutching a bloody sword. Surely Mardra had to admire her beauty, as the woman appeared to be an exact replica of her. Strewn about the feet of their visitors were five slain castle guards.

"Shit," muttered Mardra. "And I had just gotten comfortable. I believe the dark magic I just spoke of has arrived."

"Correct you are," said the old man, and began creeping

into the throne room with his lovely companion.

"A question," said Leigh to Mardra. "And I don't mean to sound…uhh, pessimistic, but is escape an option? We're warriors in training…not sorceresses. And not for nothing, did you happen to notice that chick looks just like you?"

"I can hear you just fine, young lady," said the old man, still a good hundred paces away. "And no, it is not an option. I assure you this castle is fully surrounded, and the three of you are the only breathing remnants of this little castle. You have but two choices. Death…or submission."

The old man waved his hand and the throne room doors slammed back shut. With another wave the women's weapons crashed down to the ground, and their limbs were rendered paralyzed.

*

Lillia swung her wooden sword through the open air, spinning and parrying against her imaginary attackers. These early morning swordplay sessions were the only things keeping her sane these days.

When she would sneak out to practice with her wooden blade, Landis, her vile betrothed, would still be sleeping off his drunken stupor from the night before. This morning was no exception. Perhaps if she got good enough with this wooden sword she would one day use a real one on him and flee his father's castle forever.

Underneath her heaping bosom, finely curved frame and golden blonde hair, Lillia had always been a tomboy; travelling the continent in search of danger and adventure was her calling, not the boring and repressive formality that she was stuck with due to the curse of her noble blood. If only her father, the warden of the realm's eastern territory, was at all a better man than the sniveling, maniacal brat he had traded her off to. When Lillia wasn't curtseying and faking smiles, Landis and his friends had their way with her. And when she told this to her father, he merely reminded her that if she was to be a princess, she must remember that she is property of the prince, and also that she had better not go fucking it up by getting pregnant out of wedlock and tarnishing his name.

Only when Lillia snuck out to the field beyond the castle did she have any inkling of privacy or independence. There was more to these secret outings, as well. Out here she also had a strange companion.

A couple of weeks ago, during one of these swordplay sessions, a strange figure appeared to her off in the distance. At first its presence frightened her right down to her insides. But the man or ghost or whatever he was, proved himself of a benevolent nature. In her head she'd occasionally hear him whisper words of encouragement and reassurance. Though they were always vague and cryptic, she accepted them for what they were. What more could she expect from a hooded and cloaked figure who hid off under the shadows of the forest?

Suddenly Lillia tensed as she heard obnoxious voices from off in the distance.

Away with your sword. He is coming.

"Thank you," Lillia whispered back to the hooded man.

Lillia tossed her wooden blade off into the trees and darted over to a sprouting of flowers to give off the appearance that she was just a dumb, mindless princess doing dumb and mindless princess things.

"There she is!" howled Landis, followed by three of his brutish friends. "Strip her and grab a limb, boys!"

Lillia silently cursed and awaited whatever peril was to come. This wouldn't be the first time Landis and his friends would strip and humiliate her, but it was the first time they'd caught her outside the castle where she wasn't supposed to be.

"What are you doing out here?" demanded Landis. "We had to search the castle over for your sweet little arse!"

"It was a nice morning, milord," she replied, choking back bile as she forced out the formality. "You were still asleep so I figured I'd just—"

"Shut up!" howled Landis and smacked her across the cheek. "We've got a big surprise for your daddy this morn!"

Landis tore off her dress and grabbed her large bosom with a painful squeeze.

"I'll get her legs!" growled the biggest and vilest friend of Landis, and summarily grabbed for her ankle.

Lillia might have been too afraid to hit Landis, but with these other buffoons she figured she could get away with it. As the big oaf grabbed at her ankle she lifted her foot and sent the heel of her boot down, crunching his fingers. As he jolted upright to shake off the pain she thrust her knee upward into his crotch.

Much as she had anticipated, she was then overtaken by

Landis and the other two, and could hardly defend herself with her one unrestrained limb. She may be helpless now, but she decided the little act of retaliation was well worth it, just to see that big moron down on his knees out of breath and holding his balls in agony.

"Where are you taking me?" asked Lillia in little more than a groan.

"Oh you'll see," said Landis, clutching and pulling on her arm while his fallen friend got up and hobbled over to grab Lillia's last free limb.

How Lillia wished the strange hooded man would come and save her. She did not grow angry though, for perhaps he could not do so. Ghosts and phantoms were said to be mysterious in their ways, and never appeared without reason.

Worry not, the hooded man's voice whispered in her head.

Lillia did her best to hide her reassured smile as Landis and his brutes dragged her away.

TWO

On a misty cliff overlooking the realm of Zorathustin stood two rows of mounted men, six on each side, in a bitter, cold face off. On one side sat King Rainum and his five military advisors, all of which were fierce with a sword. Across from them was Herston Maynard, the warden of the realm's eastern territory, and his five best swordsmen.

In recent weeks the in-fighting had come to a head, engendered by Maynard's burning lust to take over the throne and free his daughter from the clutches of betrothal. Young Lillia had been promised to Rainum's son in marriage before the relationship between king and warden turned sour; this would be the final negotiation before the civil war would commence.

"So we meet again, King," spat Maynard. "I'm surprised you had the sack to show up."

"And why wouldn't I, Maynard?" scoffed the king. "I appointed you as warden of the east myself. I chose you carefully, mind you. I'd not appoint an underling who could hold any perceivable threat against me. And let me assure you, your little Lillia is quite happy with her betrothed." The king whistled and snapped his fingers. "Oh, Lillia! Why don't you come out here and say hello to your father!"

From a copse of trees and brush came Rainum's son Landis, leading a terrified naked girl out by a rope that was bound about her wrists.

Rainum bellowed laughter and slapped his rotund belly as it shook over his belt like a mold of pudding. "My future daughter-in-law looking happy as ever!" he howled. "And let me tell you, my son has been enjoying her almost as much as his friends have. Haven't you, Landis?"

"Indeed, father!" hooted Landis, then smacked his nude betrothed hard on the ass.

"You are the essence of scum," hissed Maynard, but then turned his lips up into a smile. "But do you really think I'd have promised Lillia to your pathetic wretch of a son if it were her I truly cared about? My wanting to free her has nothing to do with her, you fool of a king. I need her in tact for after I kill you and take your throne, so I can pawn her off to some prince or other with a hefty sum of gold in his family's pocket.

"All the same, she is obviously now without her maidenhead, and you've given me every reason to see your rotting face on a pike. And you may think you've now gotten the best of me. Well, think again, King. I had expected you'd exploit my Lillia like this, so I've come prepared. I brought a little something with me this time…a little surprise of my own. And this little something only proves just what an unfit king you are, and just how useless your men are under your incompetent reign of madness."

"Oh, surprise me then, why don't you," laughed the king.

"While you were down in your private chambers last night, likely boozing and making your whores suffer your insufficient cock for a pittance of gold, and while your lazy guard slept through their watch, your castle was quietly infiltrated by my men. And what an easy time they had, might I add. They were already *in* your castle. Several of your guard have already sworn allegiance to me. So they had no problem slipping unseen into the royal chambers where the queen slept all by her lonesome. And here we are, some eight turns of the hourglass later, and you still don't even know she's gone. Speaking of hourglasses, Queen Arianna, why don't you come out here and show off that fine form of yours!"

Upon Maynard's whistling command a donkey rode out from the trees behind he and his men carrying Queen Arianna, who much like Maynard's daughter was nude and bound at the wrists, with the added insult of a canvas sack placed over her head.

"Horseshit!" hooted King Rainum. "You think I'd believe you could pull such a thing off? I'd recognize my own wife's body. That is obviously some common whore with a sack on her head."

"You're right about that last part, my king." Maynard brought his horse over to the queen in a casual trot and lifted the sack from her head.

"Arianna!" cried Rainum, stunned by the sight of his wife's furious face. "Are you harmed?"

"Oh, she's just fine, milord," said Maynard. "She's quite enjoyed her stay."

"That's it, Maynard," said the king. "The war begins and ends right now, right here on this very cliff. Men, draw—"

"—your swords!" cried Maynard in unison with the king.

The sound of a dozen swords being unsheathed was instantly silenced as from nowhere a mighty battle-axe lodged itself right into the face of King Rainum. Before anyone could even see from where the axe was thrown, a rather short but remarkably barrel-like man lunged downward from the cliffs above, crushing the head of Herston Maynard with a mighty blow of a war-hammer.

Every swordsman on both sides watched in stunned awe as another man, much larger, jumped from the rocks above and dislodged his axe from the dead king's split face.

"Regicide!" cried the largest and fiercest looking of the king's men. "You've killed our king! We'll have you fed to the jackals!"

"If anything," began the massive brute in a casual patter, "you'd be wise to pick that bloody crown up off the ground and place it on my head while your wives and daughters line up to join their tonsils to my prick. But, seeing as corrupt royalty is something I have a far better time slaying than actually being, I think my little friend and I will just kill the lot of you, free the girls, and be on our way."

"State your names!" cried another of the king's men.

"I am Oberyl O'Garyn of the Eerie!" shouted the little, muscular dwarf in his Eerie brogue, not to be overlooked. "Pleasure to make your acquaintances."

"And I," began the barbarian, "am Byron…of nowhere and anywhere. All depends on wherever the fuck I feel like being."

All men on both sides clutched their swords, not knowing if they should unite to kill these two or continue to fight against one another.

"Say, Byron," said the little man, "how about you take the king's men and I'll take the warden's?"

"Byron the Usurper!" gasped one of Rainum's men. "You really do exist!"

"Sounds good to me, Oberyl," replied Byron, ignoring the proclamation of Rainum's guard. "Just please don't harm any horses."

In a shocking display of agility Oberyl leaped, flipped, and hammered one of Maynard's men clear off his horse, sending him down crushed-skull-first into the dirt. Byron followed suit and beheaded the dead king's largest man with a jump and a swing of his axe.

Knowing that their horses would be of no advantage, all remaining men jumped to their feet and attacked, uniting in battle for the time being. But all was for naught, for within the span of a few short minutes Byron and Oberyl were looking down on a mangled pile of corpses and assorted body parts.

"Say, lad," Oberyl said to Byron, turning his attention to the nude girl whose wrists were bound by rope. "It just dawned on me, we killed that poor girl's father."

Byron turned to the girl, then returned his gaze back to Oberyl. "Well, no, you see…*we* didn't kill her father. *You* killed her father, my friend." Byron then looked to the naked queen perched atop the donkey. "*I* killed *her* husband and king."

"Well isn't that just like you," scoffed Oberyl. "Hogging all the credit for the slaying of a mad king and blaming me for the untimely death of some poor girl's father. I think my version of things where we share equal credit and blame is far more—"

"Oh just shut up!" cried Lillia, struggling with her rope-bound wrists. "It doesn't matter who killed who! My father and the king were both mad, treacherous, vile monsters. And now neither will kill or torture again. So I thank you both, assuming the two of you aren't as evil as the men you've just slain. Now will one of you get the fuck over here and unbind my wrists for the nine heaven's sake!"

"Of course, my dear," said Oberyl, and hurried over to the girl, trying his best not to stare at her creamy, smooth skin and golden-blonde hair. "Say, where did your betrothed bugger off to?"

"The coward turned and ran the moment you and your barbarian friend arrived," said Lillia. "Likely he's hurrying back to the castle to round up the rest of the king's men."

On the other side of the corpse pile Byron also did his best to remain gentlemanly. Delicately, he freed the nude Queen Arianna's hands and took her from the donkey, silently delighting at the feel of her soft bottom in his hand. After helping her stand on steady feet he walked her over to where Oberyl stood with Lillia.

"I too applaud you both and your actions here today,"

said the queen, sounding strong and unshaken by her recent ordeal. Byron tore away the least bloodied tunic he could find among the corpses and handed it to the queen. "Thank you, barbar," she said as she covered herself. "It can be nothing more than an act of the Nine that you happened upon this scene. In recent weeks there has been much legend told of Byron the Usurper, after that business you allegedly took care of not far south of here in Rosecrown. Some believe you are merely a myth, Byron. I myself questioned the reality of your existence, for never have I met a man who carried out justice in the name of good rather than his own perverse vanity. I thought such a man could be no more than a mythical hero."

"Well thank you, your highness…I think," said Byron, flushing about the cheeks.

"As far what took place here today on this mountainside cliff," continued the queen, "the tomes will tell of the day the mad king and his warden killed each other in battle, and Byron the Barbarian, along with his mysterious and quite adorable little friend, came by mere coincidence to the aid of the widowed queen and the warden's daughter who were left helpless for carrion. Surely I must bend the truth, otherwise you'd both be the hunt of all the king's and warden's men. People get a little bent out of shape about regicide, you know. And you've already gotten yourself quite a reputation for that."

"Sounds fair to me, your highness," said Byron.

Oberyl nodded his agreement.

"And as far as reward goes," said the queen, "I believe

that can be discussed back at the castle…preferably in my private chambers…"

*

"Are all you Eerie-men such monsters in the sheets?"

Oberyl removed his face from between Lillia's generous bosom and exhaled. He slowly extricated his lower extremity from the warmth of her dripping, cleanly shaven slit and rolled off her, his small but barrel-like frame glistening with sweat.

"No, dear," he said through breathy pants. "Just me."

Lillia laughed and rested her head on Oberyl's shoulder. "Surely you can't be the only one," she said.

"Truth be told, lass, I haven't been back to the Eerie in, well, many years. I feel as though I've forgotten more about my people than I ever knew, if such a thing be possible. I left there as a thirteen-year-old lad, got kidnapped by bandits, sold into slavery, killed my captors, and went back home five years later. Once I got back there, I felt imprisoned again, so I travelled the continent never to return."

"I would love to hear the tales of your travels," said Lillia. "I bet you've got enough stories to fill a tome."

"All that and more, my dear," laughed Oberyl.

"I find you fascinating, Eerie-man. I want to know all about Oberyl O'Garyn of the Eerie."

Oberyl reached over to Lillia's bedside table and grabbed blindly for a hog leg from the plate the serving girls had brought in earlier. He stared at the ceiling, chomping away while Lillia continued to regale him with flattery.

"Will you be staying at the castle long?" she asked.

"Doesn't look that way," he answered. "Byron and I are on a bit of a quest."

"Ooh, tell me of this quest!"

"Byron has some unfinished business south of here in Rosecrown. I swore to him that I'd assist. As much as I'd like to stay here in this very bed with you, I must be a man of my word. Byron, in the short time I've known him, has become a dear, dear friend. And also in that short time we've formed a bond that other men would take decades to build. His fate shall be mine to share."

"You are a devoted one, Oberyl." Lillia's soft fingers grazed across Oberyl's chest, sliding slowly down to his cock which began to stiffen, so soon after having just been spent. "I do love that in a man."

"You're but a young lass, Lillia," scoffed Oberyl, and took another massive bite off the hog leg. "How old are you?"

"Nineteen," she said. "I'm no lass."

"Perhaps not, but still a babe to my old eyes. And of noble blood. What could you possibly see in sawed-off miniature barbarian like me with hog juice dripping down his chin? Shouldn't you be off chasing princes?"

"You might remember just this morning I had a prince. Or shall I say, he had me…bound at the wrists at his cruel mercy."

"For fuck's sake, I forgot about him!" cried Oberyl, flushing about the face. "If we're caught..."

"Relax," said Lillia. "He had little interest in me beyond

making me his plaything. And anyways, Queen Arianna has assured me that he is now as good as a bastard. When we returned this morning he was already claiming himself king. Arianna was having none of it. He wasn't even her child, you know. And she's hated him since the day she married her late king. I was told he fled the castle."

"Well, that's refreshing," said Oberyl.

"And now Queen Arianna will likely appoint me some noble position in either this castle or my dead father's east of here. But I'd trade that in in a heartbeat to travel the continent like you and Byron. I've no interest in sissy princes and all the formality that comes with this life. It's no life at all, if you ask me."

"I can't say I disagree, dear," said Oberyl. "But look at this room! You've got the comfiest bed I've ever set myself upon. A hearth. Serving girls at your beck and call."

"And a future planned by others than myself," said Lillia, growing irritated. "I've always been a bit of a tomboy. I was practicing swords while all the other little girls were out picking daisies and dreaming of princes. I want out!"

A knock pounded against the bedchamber door.

"Hold on!" cried Lillia, lifting the blankets to cover her and her naked lover. "Come in!"

The door creaked open and in strode Byron, laughing at the sight.

"Eating in bed, Oberyl?" he scoffed.

"This pork is to die for, barbarian," laughed Oberyl. "Why don't you hop in here and join us?"

"No thank you," groaned Byron over Lillia's pleasant

laughter. "Come now. The celebration is about to begin, and you and I are apparently the guests of honor."

*

The celebration was in full swing, but the two guests of honor stood out on the terrace overlooking the moonlit river, taking a quiet moment to figure out their next move.

"Quite a party," said Oberyl, leaning up against the balustrade with a pipe hanging from his lips and a massive stein of ale in his hand. "But why the hells did you drag me out here to stare at the water? Don't you hate the stuff?"

"I hate being in it or floating in a boat above it," said Byron. "But you can't say this isn't a nice view."

"Sure is," grunted Oberyl. "But what's a nicer view are the tits popping out of every bodice in the ballroom. Full sized women sure are intrigued by this little Eerie-man, which I think you noticed upon your rather rude intrusion before the party. My, that Lillia sure is something."

"She's a lovely girl," agreed Byron. "And what a set of tits."

"I thought you'd notice that," laughed Oberyl. "Speaking of which, you aren't in that big of a hurry to get back to Rosecrown, are you?"

"Need I remind you, little friend, of our journey's importance?" said Byron, still staring out at the horizon as though looking for something out there in the dark waters. "And need I also remind you what you said to me as we departed Mount Valgorn? Do you not remember one of your rare moments of emotion, after punching me in the nuts, when you swore you'd fight by my side till your dying day?"

"Or until I found a rich princess or kingless queen to marry," said Oberyl, cutting Byron off. "Yes, I remember it well. And I'm still here, aren't I? I could very well have stayed in the woods with Phadriel and lived out the rest of my days in sexually sated bliss with my ebon goddess. But here I am, sharing the spoils of victory with you yet again. I meant what I said to you, barbar. We make a great team, and I'm by your side for as long as you'll have me. All I'm saying right now is… I banged Lillia three goddamn times before this party even started. And, you've been given numerous sexual advances from Queen Arianna, which I'm assuming you accepted. And let's not forget there are a gaggle of giddy girls in there who're more than happy to tongue our—"

"Yes, there certainly are, Oberyl!" spat Byron, finally turning to look down at his friend. "And there's no doubt you'll enjoy them all before you pass out tonight. All *I'm* saying is that—"

"Stop speaking!" cried Oberyl. "It just dawned on me! You're sober! You've not had a single drink all night. And while I was ravaging the warden's daughter this afternoon and getting massaged by the castle girls, you weren't even taking the queen up on her offers of reward, were you, lad?"

Byron groaned and turned his gaze back out to the dark horizon.

"Hah!" hooted Oberyl. "Got a conscience now all of a sudden, do ya', boy?"

"You know, little man," began Byron as he turned his

gaze back down upon his little friend, "if you were any other man I'd have killed you by now."

Oberyl finished his ale in one massive gulp and slammed the stein down on the balustrade. After letting out a thunderous belch he looked up and met Byron's eyes.

Byron was taken aback by the look his friend was giving him. Not only did it seem that Oberyl was about to show another of his rare displays of emotion, but the look on the Eerie-man's face was one of wisdom and experience. Byron had never inquired about Oberyl's age, but at that moment his little friend looked years, decades even, older than Byron. Suddenly, it seemed to make sense how the little man always referred to him as lad or boy.

"You know, Byron," began Oberyl in a thoughtful tone, "I had a Mardra once. Many years ago. Or at least I thought I did."

"What happened to her?" asked Byron.

"Well, there's a lot you don't know about me, laddie. There's much I haven't told you. Yet."

"Tell me, then."

"There'll be time for you to hear the telling of my life story in the days and years to come. Let's not get off track. The point I'm trying to make is that I was once a fool in love, much like yourself. Her name was Greta."

"An Eerie-girl?" asked Byron.

"Heavens no," laughed Oberyl. "The only Eerie-girl I've ever lain with was a whore that I paid for as a rebound fuck after things went south with Greta."

"So who was this Greta?"

“A princess, lad.” said Oberyl. “Well, she was then. Now she’s a queen.”

“A queen?” Byron searched his mind for a moment. “I’ve heard of a Queen Greta, just south of the Eerie, actually. She’s the Queen of Vladaria.”

“Yup,” said Oberyl, nodding.

“But she’s been queen since long before I was even born! Sixty some-odd years, at least. She has to be over eighty!”

“Your blind guesses at history and aging serve you fairly well, barbar,” laughed Oberyl. “She’s been queen since she was eighteen years of age, the year 2208 of the Unnamed Continent Under the Nine Gods.”

“Which was exactly sixty years ago,” said Byron. “Which would make her seventy-eight.”

“That is correct,” said Oberyl.

“And how old are you, actually, Eerie-man?”

“I too am seventy-eight.”

“Gods,” gasped Byron. “You don’t look a day over thirty. Thirty-five, maybe.”

“Why thank you,” said Oberyl, laughing heartily. “There’s a reason for that too, Byron. But that’s a tale to be quilled in another tome.”

“And how exactly does an Eerie-man end up with a princess?” asked Byron.

“Because he’s a damn good looking Eerie-man with an ogre-sized cock, is how.” Oberyl reached for his ale stein, forgetting he’d emptied it only moments ago, and turned back to Byron. “And I wasn’t just an Eerie-man then, mind you. I was a slave under her stepfather King Ezryn.

Technically, though, I was her stepbrother's property. But that didn't last long. I killed him…and his friends, and ran away with Greta. We were in love, or so I thought."

"And what happened?"

"The specifics aren't important, and we've gotten way off track here. What is important, and what I was trying to say, is that I know how you feel, lad. I will still bust your balls about it, you whiny, pathetic excuse for a barbarian. But just know that I understand, as I was once a young fool like yourself. And when I was, I'd have risked everything for Greta, just like you would, and do, for this Mardra girl. So in the morning, when my head is pounding, my throat is dry, and my nearly eighty-year-old loins are exhausted, we will ride out for Rosecrown, as much as I'd like to stay."

"You are a good man, Oberyl O'Garyn of the Eerie."

"I know," laughed Oberyl. "But tell me, what were you doing all day if not fucking the queen?"

Byron turned his gaze back to the horizon. "You remember her son, the one who had Lillia on a rope at the melee this morning?"

"Ahh, yes. Sniveling little shit."

"I was in talks with Queen Arianna and her men about the likelihood of where he had gone after he fled the castle this morning," said Byron. "A small boat was missing from the docks when we got here today. The queen guesses that he sailed down to the other end of the river where the late Maynard held watch over the east."

"And," began Oberyl, "you guessed he'd tell them the king is dead and the castle is his…not to mention that you were also the guy who killed him, and that they were now his men."

"Correct. And that we should expect them to storm the castle tonight, demanding all to bow to that little fuck or be killed," said Byron.

Oberyl hoisted himself up onto the balustrade and looked out into the horizon.

"Your Eerie-man vision seeing anything that I don't see?" asked Byron.

Oberyl focused hard for a moment and jumped back down onto the terrace. "Four boats anchored about three miles out," he said. "Four that I could see, at least. Shall we go warn the queen?"

"Sure," said Byron. "But first, I guess I'll have a drink."

*

Less than one turn of the hourglass later Byron and Oberyl stood on the shore, axe and hammer at the ready. Behind them were Queen Arianna's men, some five hundred strong. Much like Oberyl, most of the queen's men were well into their cups, but also much like Oberyl, the alcohol seemed only to sharpen their skills, as well as add fun to the oncoming fight. The approaching ships were now clearly in view; the sound of fingers clutching hilts sounded high in the air.

"Come on already," grunted Byron. "I've places to be."

"Patience, barbar," laughed Oberyl. "Mardra likely isn't going anywhere in the next day. You can wait. Besides, this shouldn't take long. We've got an actual army behind us."

"That's a first," said Byron. "Who'd have ever thunk it? The most wanted man on the continent leading a royal army to the fight."

Waiting for Oberyl to respond, Byron looked down at his friend to find him staring up at the mountains to the east of the river.

"What is it?" asked Byron.

"Not sure," Oberyl replied. "For a moment I thought I saw—"

The Eerie-man's reply was cut short by the sound of a catapult being released from one of the ships. Shields were raised and arrows were cocked, but withdrawn as the approaching projectile revealed itself to be nothing more than the corpse of Landis, the late King Rainum's now equally late son.

"Serves him right," said Byron as Landis's body thumped down onto the sand. "But with king, prince and warden now all dead, it begs the question: who exactly are we defending the throne for?"

"You aren't," came the voice of the queen from behind Byron and Oberyl.

The duo turned to find Queen Arianna standing before an entire army's worth of swords and arrows pointed directly at them.

"But how?" demanded Byron.

"Your youth and inexperience are evident, barbar," said Queen Arianna. "I had plenty of time to send messengers east. Maynard's men took no time deciding to bow to me, knowing they'd go down in the tomes of history as the men who captured Byron the Usurper."

"Told you you should've just fucked her, Byron," laughed Oberyl.

"And you, dwarf," hissed the queen. "Your fate will be no better than your friend's. Especially after that remark."

"You're making a big mistake," gasped Byron.

"Oh, and you can't expect me to believe your fool story that you're simply headed to Rosecrown to reclaim a lost love," said Arianna. "Word from my scouts came just this afternoon about what your false queen has done."

"What in the Nine are you talking about?" asked Byron.

"Mardra was no better than the mad queen you killed to get her the throne. She slayed her entire castle, I was told. And now you're, what, on your way there to slay the entire territory and take the crown by her side?"

"Queen Arianna," began Byron, "I urge you to reconsider this, for you are wrong, and you are forcing me to do something I swore I would never do."

"What? Surrender?" cried the queen with a smirk. "You might as well, barbarian. Rosecrown will be mine. So go on, break your foolish oath and take a knee."

"Oh no, my queen," said Byron. "Surrendering is not of what I speak."

"Then what?" asked the queen.

"Killing a woman!" cried Byron as his axe screamed through the air and parted Queen Arianna's head from its shoulders.

Oberyl hooted an unintelligible battle cry and began hammering flat the heads of the surrounding soldiers, smiling ear to ear as blood, brain and skull flew. Byron followed suit, his axe and mace spinning like tornados of steel and crimson flesh.

The duo fought their way through the hordes of soldiers, making quick work of each and every man that came their way, despite being vastly outnumbered.

"So what's our goal here?" asked Oberyl nonchalantly as he and Byron found themselves backed up against the wall of the castle.

"Survive, I guess," said Byron, carelessly tearing down soldier after soldier.

"We must rescue the girl," said Oberyl, then spit as a chunk of bone and brain splattered against his face.

Byron's laugh almost cost him an ear as he was momentarily distracted; he quickly made up for it by beheading three men in a row with three simple jerks of his axe.

"There you go again, Oberyl," laughed Byron.

"What?!" demanded the Eerie-man defensively.

"Falling for every girl you dip your quill in. How do you know she's not part of this setup?"

"I just know," said Oberyl. "A man can read a woman well when he's lain with her. It's something in her eyes, I believe."

"What a festering load of mule shit that is," laughed Byron.

"Say, Byron, I don't think we can stay backed up against this wall forever. Got any plans for actually getting out of this alive?"

Byron thought as he fought, but found no answers. “No,” he finally said. “But hey, you never finished telling me what you saw up on the mountain. You know, before the dead son of the king came flying at us.”

“Ahh yes,” said Oberyl. “Looked like a strange man. Hooded and cloaked. Like a wizard or something.”

“We could certainly use a wizard right about now,” said Byron. “There must be six hundred strong still coming at us.”

“Which reminds me, you haven’t been keeping count, have you?”

“’fraid not, little man.”

“Oh well, we’ll just call this one a draw.”

“Five hundred and one!” laughed Byron as he took the next man down with his axe.

“Oh no you don’t!” cried Oberyl, doubling his efforts.

The barbarian and the Eerie-man continued on hacking limbs and crushing skulls while planning a way out of their corner. An idea struck Byron when arrows started flying. Looking up, he noticed an arrow soar over his head and through an open castle window.

“How strong are you, little man?” asked the barbarian.

“I think you must know me well enough by now,” replied Oberyl.

“Well, let me rephrase that. Are you strong enough to give me ten fingers?”

“Ten fingers up your arse? I think that’s a question of your strength, not mine.”

“Making joke at my expense, even in the face of almost certain death,” laughed Byron. “I hardly find that appropriate."

"Again, Byron, I think you must know me well enough by now."

"In a few seconds I'm going to lift my foot up, then you're going to give it a push, then you're going to grab my leg as fast as you can."

Byron's foot was up before Oberyl could even respond, and with a mighty thrust Oberyl hoisted him into the air with every last ounce of his might. Oberyl grabbed for Byron's leg as fast as he could, and found himself dangling from Byron, who was hanging by one hand from the castle window.

"Mighty fine predicament you've landed us in here, barbarian!" howled Oberyl, doing his best to deflect arrows with his mighty hammer.

"Tell me about it!" Byron hollered back. "Just give me a moment here. If I don't get an arrow up my ass I'll pull this off."

"If you do pull this off I just might reward you with those ten fingers I offered!"

With one mighty heave Byron hoisted himself up over the bottom of the window and slid in with Oberyl safely behind him.

"Take a breather, shall we?" said Byron as he sank into a sitting position against the wall next to the open window.

"Mighty fine idea, barbarian," replied Oberyl with a heavy sigh, seating himself beside Byron. "But what's next?"

"Hide?" Byron suggested.

"I doubt that'll last long," said Oberyl. "We don't know

this castle as well as they do."

"You are of sound logic, Eerie-man," groaned Byron.

"I can hide you," came a voice from outside the room. Lillia popped her head in through the doorway. "Come quickly!"

"And how do I know we can trust you, girl?" asked Byron.

"You don't," replied Lillia. "But the way I see it, I'm the only chance you've got."

"She's right, Byron," said Oberyl. "And believe me, we can trust her."

"Well, are you two going to sit there and wait for death, or are you going to come with me?" asked Lillia. "Since my father sent me here I've learned a thing or two about hiding."

"Right then," said Byron. "Let's go."

The duo scrambled up to their feet and hurried out of the room behind Lillia.

"Where are you taking us?" asked Byron.

"Beneath the castle," the girl replied as they hurried down the hallway. "There are tunnels, several of them. One leads to my dead betrothed's secret pleasure chamber. None knew of it but he and the king. And well, me and the castle whores. Beyond that cursed room is a way out behind the castle."

"But…" began Byron, "behind the castle there is only water."

"Right," said Lillia as she stopped at a massive oak door. "Grab a sconce from the wall. These tunnels are dark."

"But if behind the castle lies the river, how do we

escape?" asked Byron.

"By boat, you idiot!" hissed Lillia as she heaved the door open on her own. "Now grab a fucking sconce and follow me or we're all dead!"

Byron coughed as Oberyl gave him a hard elbow to the ribs.

"Suck it up," laughed Oberyl. "Time for you to brave the high seas again. If you're really as pathetic on a boat as you've told me, this is going to make for one entertaining ride!"

"Come on!" shouted Lillia from halfway down the stairs.

Byron and Oberyl followed as Lillia led them through the dark subterranean mazes that finally brought them to her late fiancé's cursed pleasure chamber. Lillia removed a sconce from the wall which triggered a false door to open, revealing a short hallway with a steel door at its end.

"The late prince had this false door installed to sneak whores in and out of the castle unseen," said Lillia. "So don't forget to send him a prayer of thanks."

Beyond the door was a stone stairway that led down to a small dock where a simple rowboat was tied.

"We're escaping in that?" groaned Byron.

"You'd prefer death?" asked Lillia.

"Pardon my ungrateful friend, please, dear Lillia," laughed Oberyl.

"Of course," laughed the girl. "Now let's be off."

"She's coming with us?" Byron said to Oberyl.

"I am!" Lillia shot back at the barbarian. "And there's nothing you can do about it, unless you would choose to stay and die."

"So be it," groaned Byron.

*

Oberyl rowed the small boat while Lillia tried to comfort Byron, whose head was dangling over the side, green with seasickness.

"Get yourself together, will you!" hissed Oberyl. "We're not out of danger's way yet."

Byron responded with grunt and a gurgle.

"I think he'll be all right," laughed Lillia. "Once he finally wretches he'll probably get his sea legs."

"Well at least try and keep yourself from puking until we're well beyond sight and sound," added Oberyl.

The boat came to a fork in the river, just beyond the castle. Byron and Oberyl turned to see the battleships still anchored, and further on the shore where six hundred or so kingless and queenless men were still storming the castle in search of them.

"Byron," whispered Oberyl, pointing to the mountains. "Do you see him?"

Byron forced himself so sit up and stop swaying enough to focus his vision on the mountains.

"There, up top," said Oberyl. "The hooded man."

"Yes," groaned Byron. "He's still there. Looks like a wizard, all right. Can you see his face? My eyes are a little…blurry."

"No. It's shrouded under his hood. But I can tell you one thing, he can definitely see us. He's looking right at us."

Byron vomited and slumped down into the boat.

"I believe it's me he's watching," said Lillia over the sound of Byron's puking.

Byron and Oberyl each did a double take.

"You know him?" asked Byron, wiping vomit off his chin.

"He first appeared a couple weeks ago," said Lillia. "When I'd be out in the courtyard practicing with my sword I'd see him off in the distance. Each time I spotted him he'd vanish shortly after."

"Did he ever speak to you?" asked Byron.

"Sort of," replied Lillia. "His communication was telepathic."

"Is he telling you anything right now?" asked Oberyl.

"Right now he is silent," said Lillia. "But trust me, he's on our side. Mine, at least."

The trio sailed on into the darkness for the better part of an hour, guided by the nearly burnt out torches they had escaped from the castle with.

"Say, Byron," began Oberyl, "I almost forgot to mention this. Before you axed the queen you said you swore you'd never kill a woman."

"Correct," said Byron.

"Well, I'm just a tad puzzled as I seem to remember you telling me you killed the mad queen of Rosecrown."

"That's, well, different," reasoned Byron. "I mean, sure, she had the plumbing of a woman, but she was an evil sorceress. That doesn't count."

"Sounds noble enough to me," said Lillia.

"Plus, I just really thought it would be great to say such a thing before I did it," added Byron.

"I can't argue with that," said Oberyl. "It definitely got my fighting spirit up and ready."

"Anyhow," said Byron, "I suppose now is as good a time as any to talk about that bit of news the queen dropped on us before I chopped her head off."

"Do you believe it?" asked Oberyl.

"Believe what?" asked Lillia.

"The queen claimed her scouts reported that the woman we're on our way to see, my lost love, if you will, went mad and slayed her entire castle."

"Well, do you believe it?" asked Lillia.

"I believe the castle was slain, sure," said Byron. "But no, I do not believe it was her."

"I doubt she would do that," said Lillia.

"How would you know?" asked Byron.

"I met her once."

"You met Mardra!" cried Byron. "You actually saw her? How? When?"

"She was a guest at the castle just weeks ago. She was perhaps the nicest and humblest queen I've ever met. A lot of fun too. And her friends, Leigh and Lynette I believe their names were. Just delightful the three of them."

"I can't believe this," said Byron. "Did she look well?"

"Lovely woman," replied Lillia. "And without a king. I can't imagine any man would be stupid enough to turn down an offer of being her groom and king."

"Why don't we stop this conversation right there,"

laughed Oberyl. "You both seem to agree that she didn't slay her castle. So the question remains, who did and how."

"Well, I can't help but think that shape shifting demon we encountered after the business at Castle Valgorn might have had something to do with it."

"Ahh yes," laughed Oberyl. "The one who turned you into a—"

"No need to retell that story," said Byron flatly.

"Turned you into what?" asked Lillia.

"Not important," Byron insisted. "What's important is that we get to Rosecrown as fast as…"

"As fast as what?" said Oberyl.

"Listen," said Byron. "Do you hear that?"

The trio looked around into the dark night.

"It sounds like boiling water," said Oberyl.

"I don't believe rivers are supposed to do that," said Byron as steam began rising from around the boat.

"Shit!" cried Oberyl as the river beneath them came to a rolling boil and burning water splashed up against them.

"Row ashore!" Byron cried. "Quickly!"

Frantically Oberyl rowed and rowed, cursing and shouting against the fiery hot spray.

At last they reached the shore and jumped out onto the land.

There, up close and in person, they found themselves standing before the hooded man.

"Is this some dark magic!" cried Byron, unsheathing his axe from its holster on his back.

"Answer the man!" added Oberyl, doing the same with

his war hammer.

"I too would like to know what you're all about," said Lillia. "And just who the fuck are you exactly?"

The hooded man said nothing, only stood before them with his arms folded within his brown cloak.

"If you won't speak, at least show your face," said Byron.

At last a response came from the hooded man, but it was no more than a laugh.

"We're on a very important mission," said Byron. "If you stopped us like you did just to play games, I urge you to let us be back on our way."

"It doesn't seem to me you can sail very far in a boiling river, Byron," the hooded man finally spoke. His tone sounded like that of a much younger man than they had expected to be hiding under that hood, yet something in the man's voice sounded eerily familiar to Byron.

"You know who I am?" asked Byron.

"I know you quite well barbarian," the man replied. "And who exactly is this mission important to?" Byron gave no answer. "Just as I thought. A mission important only to yourself. Off to reclaim the girl that you let get away. Some barbarian you are."

"It's not just that!" demanded Byron. "Well, maybe it was at first, but, look, I've been told that—"

"That your former lover Mardra went mad and slayed her entire castle? Yes, I heard that too."

"Then you must understand the importance with which we travel," said Byron. "Something has happened to her. We must find out what, and restore the greatness of her name."

"Oh, I do understand," said the hooded man.

"Then why the fuck did you stop us like that?" asked Oberyl.

"Two reasons," said the man. "One, the fate of Lillia here does not lie with the two of you. At least not at the moment. Her duties lie elsewhere right now."

"What do you know of my duties?" spat Lillia. "My fate is my own to decide. I left the life of others making decisions for me behind in that cursed castle."

"I do not dispute you on that matter, dear," said the man.

"Then what do you know of my fate?"

The hooded man gave no answer.

"And what was the second reason you stopped us?" asked Byron.

"The second reason I stopped you, you buffoon, is that you were going the wrong way."

"Well then," began Byron, "what do you say you just lower the heat on the river there and point us back in the right direction?"

The hooded man again responded with mere laughter.

A mighty splash sounded from the boiling river behind them. Byron and Oberyl raised their weapons and turned to find a monstrous creature of the water come flying out screeching and wailing in deafening anguish.

The two warriors assumed the battle stance as the giant monstrosity of gills, tentacles and scaly flesh plummeted to the ground.

A tentacle came flying at Byron, which he dodged and

gave a good slice with his axe, but failed to make a cut.

"Ouch!" cried the monster in a gurgling human tongue.

Oberyl charged and tried to pound the body of the creature with his hammer, but was snatched up by another tentacle and left hanging upside down.

"Stop!" cried the monster. "Please, I mean you no harm!"

The monster dropped Oberyl to the ground and relaxed its many tentacles.

"What are you?" asked Byron.

"Just a simple sea monster," it replied, short of breath. "Really, I have no desire to hurt either of you."

"Then why in the nine hells did you come flying at us like that?" demanded Oberyl.

"Uhh, hello, my home is boiling," the monster replied. "If your house caught on fire would you just sit there and wait it out?"

"No, I suppose not," replied Oberyl.

"We figured you were a warrior of this wizard here," said Byron.

"What wizard?" asked the monster.

Byron and Oberyl turned to find both the hooded man and Lillia were gone.

"Shit," muttered Byron.

"A shit wizard?" asked the monster.

"Never mind," said Byron. "Say, you wouldn't happen to know how to get to Rosecrown, would you?"

"Rosecrown, of course," said the monster. "That's not far at all."

"We need to get there as soon as possible, uhh, what's your name?" asked Oberyl.

"Glordak," said the monster. "Say, it looks like my home stopped boiling. If you guys want to hop on my back, I could give you a ride."

"Give us a ride?" asked Byron.

"Sure! Just hop on my back and I can have you guys in Rosecrown by dawn."

Byron sized up the monster. He was easily ten feet tall, and at least seven feet wide. More than adequate for travelling on.

"Well, if you don't mind," said Byron, "that would be great. And maybe you could stick close to the shallow waters?"

"All right then, I suppose," said Glordak. "Let's get moving."

Glordak jumped high in the air and landed back in the river with a splash.

"I must say," began Oberyl as the duo walked over to their awaiting water chariot, "this seems to have worked out far better than I thought."

"Indeed," agreed Byron.

"But what of Lillia?"

"I'm not too worried," said Byron. "I can't help but think that strange wizard was, in a very sick and twisted wizardly way, trying to help us."

THREE

Byron and Oberyl trotted on horseback toward the rim of the the Forest of Torianne, nearing the town square. Glordak had made good on his offer of carrying them on his back to the rim of Rosecrown, not far from where the Forest of Torianne began. The duo even managed to score a couple hours of peaceful, uninterrupted sleep along the way. After touching down on land they had acquired two horses by means they were not necessarily proud of, but the stable owner would be paid back in one way or another, should Byron and Oberyl complete their mission alive.

For Byron, their arrival had been empty and devoid of the excitement he had expected it would bring. His mind was cluttered; his heart racing. What exactly had happened last night? Who was the elusive yet oddly helpful hooded man? Best not dwell on it, he thought. Who or whatever had set the waters of the river aboil was clearly not working against him.

When the duo had passed the dirt road where only months ago Byron had bested a dirt dweller in combat, he hoped Groozelak would pop up from the ground and greet them. With the creature's absence came a twinge of despair; something was missing. The forest was too quiet; the ground was too still.

And where was Teela? Surely the centaurs had to have been watching, ready to bid him welcome.

And when the duo had come upon the very sentimental spot in the woods where an arrow had once flown by Byron's head and a masked assassin then tried to kill him, his heart felt too empty even to ache. Surely she had not gone mad and slain her entire castle. So what exactly would be waiting for him when he got there?

"The town square is not far, friend," said Byron. "Just a bit further down this path."

"Nine heavens, lad," said Oberyl. "Those are the first words you've uttered since we entered the realm this morning. You've got a premonition?"

"What makes you ask that?" Byron grabbed for his canteen, took a long gulp, and set it back in its holster. "When you look at me, do you see a seer, Eerie-man?"

"The only thing I see right now is a bunch of trees and the biggest mope of a barbarian on the continent." Oberyl paused to let out a bellowing laugh. "When you're quiet it means one of two things, lad. Either you sense trouble, or you're still crying inside over this Mardra girl…that Mardra *queen*, rather…sorry. And seeing as we're less than an hour from where she sits, I had to assume it's the former."

"Call it a bit of both, Oberyl. Yes, we are much less than an hour from where she sits. But I do indeed sense trouble. And something tells me she's not going to be greeting us when we arrive. But what, I wonder, will be there in her place?"

"Ever the pessimist, aren't you?" scoffed Oberyl. "I know what you're doing. You're just planning for the worst, so when you show up and find her lips wrapped around the cock of some other barbarian you won't be as disappointed."

Byron cast his friend an icy stare. "You're lucky I like you, little man."

"And you're lucky I like you enough to let you call me little man and not murder you," laughed Oberyl. "But really, we've come all this way from Valgorn. Hundreds of grueling miles by foot and horseback, and you can't just be happy we've finally arrived. My balls are aching, dammit."

"This land, this air…it doesn't feel like it did when I was last here, Oberyl. When I was last here the forest might have been dying, but now it feels completely dead. The air is stale. There is no wind at our backs. This forest should be lush with life now. I feel only death."

"You sure are a tough nut to crack, barbar," said Oberyl, then pointed off into the distance ahead of them. "I see a break in the greenery. Are those buildings over there?"

"Yes, at last!" boomed Byron and sped his horse's gallop.

The duo sped through the hundred-or-so paces to the end of the forest, but quickly pulled on the reigns as they came upon what should have been civilization.

"Perhaps you truly are a seer, Byron," said Oberyl, stunned by the sight before him.

"No, my friend," began Byron, "I just have a good nose

for death."

Byron and Oberyl dismounted their suddenly restless horses, and instead of tying them to trees they allowed them to run free back into the woods, hopefully all the way back to their stable so their owner would be none the wiser. It would be easy enough to find a pair of horses to bring them further on this journey, should the journey even lead them back out of Rosecrown. The abundance of blood and death that lay sprawled out around them on the stone streets made them question the likelihood of that happenstance.

Stepping over heaps of slain bodies, Byron found one he recognized. "Selani," he said, and knelt down to hold the dead woman's hand. "The finest boar legs in Rosecrown." Byron waited for a response from Oberyl but heard nothing. "Oberyl?!" He looked around and found his companion standing by the overturned cart that had once been the dead girl's livelihood, biting away at a massive boar leg and not being bashful about the sauce that covered his face. "Really, Oberyl!"

The Eerie-man swallowed quickly and wiped his mouth with his massive trunk of a forearm. "Yes?" Byron remained on one knee, and shot Oberyl an icy glare. "Oh…I take it you knew that one." Oberyl discarded the now bare bone and made his way over the corpses to comfort his friend.

"A true Eerie-man," groaned Byron. "I kneel here honoring the dead, and you're stuffing your face."

"My apologies, friend," said Oberyl. "But for fuck's sake, man. We got into the territory at dawn and haven't eaten since last night. And that was the damn finest boar leg

I've ever had!"

"Thank Selani here," said Byron. "She made it."

Oberyl knelt on one knee and closed his eyes. He began speaking in a tongue Byron had not heard before, almost as if he were chanting.

"What was that?" asked Byron.

"An old Eerie prayer," said Oberyl, then rose to his feet. "Well Wishes for the Dead, it roughly translates to in the common tongue."

"You pray?" scoffed Byron.

"Not exactly, lad," laughed Oberyl. "For the Eerie-folk a prayer is more of a wishing of good luck upon others. Most of us folks don't believe in the nine gods. Old Eerie legend says that you could see the heavens from the highest peak of the Eerie. In truth, you see nothing above you but clouds, and if you look around, you see nothing but dive-taverns and cheap whorehouses. We lost our spiritual side many generations ago."

"I think I could retire to that old home of yours someday," laughed Byron, then rose to his feet. "Could be interesting bedding a whore I'm twice the size of. Anyways, the question remains, how did an entire town square suddenly drop dead?"

"Doesn't look to me like they just dropped dead, my friend," said Oberyl. "Look at them. Some of them are cut up to ribbons. There aren't just bodies strewn about this street, but body *parts*. Arms, legs, even heads. These folks were massacred."

"Say, Oberyl," began Byron, "that boar leg you were

eating…was it still hot?"

"Fairly warm," said Oberyl. "Plenty left over there too. I'm still quite hungr—"

"Just as I thought," said Byron, cutting Oberyl off. "Selani's hand was still warm. This siege couldn't have happened more than an hour ago."

"So the cause of it couldn't have gotten very far," said Oberyl.

"Precisely," said Byron.

"That would probably explain *that*," said Oberyl, pointing his finger to the north.

Byron looked up the road and found a massive horde of goblins approaching.

"How many would you estimate there are?" asked the Eerie-man.

"I'm not good at making estimations," laughed Byron. "Best we just take out our weapons and keep a running count of the ones we kill, and tally them at the end."

"This little contest again!" Oberyl laughed and hooted in delight. "See ya' at the end!" Oberyl unsheathed his hammer and ran right into the oncoming mob, immediately crushing three goblin heads with ease.

"Wait up!" cried Byron.

*

Surrounded by a sea of dead, pig-faced goblins, as well as the many slain townsfolk of Rosecrown, Byron and Oberyl were each seated on Selani's overturned cart, taking a breather and replenishing their energy with a victory meal of boar legs.

"Thirty-seven," said Byron, then took a massive bite of pig flesh.

Oberyl grunted and pursed his lips. "Thirty-five," he admitted. "You may have won this battle, barbarian. But the war is far from over."

The duo sat in thoughtful silence for a moment until Byron suddenly tensed and said, "You know, something just occurred to me."

"And what pray tell might that be?" asked Oberyl.

"How long ago was it that we slayed Zaltara?"

"*We* slayed?" Oberyl paused to chuckle. "You mean how long ago did Mistria the mighty dragon slay Zaltara."

"Fine, whatever," said Byron. "That's not the point I was getting to."

"Well, let's see. We reached Rosecrown this morning after our incident in Zorathustin yesterday. Before that we trailed through Strygaria for two days. Before that we spent eleven long days riding around the channel because you refused to spend three stinking days aboard a ship, pussy. And before that we spent about three days riding from Mount Valgorn through Peacebrook, Westmyrh…a time I'll forever remember, and then Leedonia. So all together that puts our departure from Valgorn…sixteen days ago."

"Odd," said Byron.

"Why is that?"

"Aside from that debacle at Westmyrh and our battle at Zorathustin yesterday, we've had a pretty uneventful trip.

And our destination just happens to get sacked and slaughtered by Goblins a mere hour before we get here."

"Interesting indeed, now that you mention it, Byron. It almost seems as if they timed it perfectly. And you did say that that old demon master guy in Westmyrh gave you some cryptic warning. I seem to remember you telling me so as you were hobbling into my room with your pants around your ankles right before I shot my—"

"Yes I remember it too!" shouted Byron, turning red about the face. "You need not remind me. I'm of a mind to believe that the old demon master has something to do with all of this."

"Could very well be."

"He's a master of demons, though. Or just one, as far as we know. Not goblins."

"Goblins are demons, Byron. Very low in the race, mindless creatures they are, but demons all the same. Either way, I don't think it would be hard for some evil, powerful wizard to command a small or even a large army of them."

"But why would he just throw goblins at us? Surely he must know that my axe and your hammer combined with our fighting skills would make quick work of a goblin horde three times the size of what lay sprawled out and decapitated before us."

"He did not mean to kill us," said Oberyl. "A simple distraction or obstacle, perhaps."

"But why?

"To keep us from getting somewhere, I'd imagine. And we're headed to Mardra's castle…whatever he's trying to keep us from is probably happening—"

"I can't believe we've wasted the last few moments sitting here on our asses!" cried Byron as he burst up onto his feet and darted away.

"Precisely," said Oberyl. "Wait up!"

*

The people of the castle, as had been reported by Queen Arianna, had met the same fates as the commonfolk of Rosecrown. Around the castle they lay sprawled out in lifelessness. A small band of goblins guarded the castle, but were quick to fall as the barbarian and the Eerie-man stormed through them with axe and hammer.

The interior of the castle was no different, and the few goblins that made a feeble attempt of denying Byron and Oberyl entry to the throne room were quickly turned to bloody shreds of black, hairy flesh. Byron found himself hoping for a greater challenge, for maybe such a thing could distract him from the memories that flooded his heart upon setting foot in the castle.

"So which way to the throne room?" asked Oberyl, grunting and panting in hope for more action.

"Straight ahead and to the right, friend," said Byron.

"And if your love isn't there?"

"We'll jump off that bridge when we come to it, little man. Now let's go!"

The duo charged down the hall, worried more about slipping on puddles of blood than the weapon-wielding goblins that got in their way. As they reached the throne room doors they each jump-kicked their way through. Both halted and drew their weapons cautiously as they found the throne room's new ghostly inhabitant.

"Welcome, Byron," said a spectral form of the old demon master, standing next to Mardra's overturned throne. "You must remember me."

"Azar," said Byron. "How could I ever forget?" Byron raised his axe and clutched his fingers tightly around its hilt.

"You need not take up arms, Byron," said Azar's apparition. "For surely you realize my physical body is not here. Nor is your dearest Mardra. I fear she is now far, far from here."

"And wherever she may be, do you really think we'll not find her?" piped in Oberyl.

"No, little man. I do not."

"I've seen every corner of this continent, demon master. Long before my barbarian friend here even took up an axe for the first time, I was crushing scum like you under my hammer."

"Well don't the two of you just make a lovely team. But oh, there is not an ounce of magic between the two of you. A human ape and a dwarf from the mountains of the Eerie."

"I am not a dwarf!" howled Oberyl.

"I know, I know," scoffed Azar. "An Eerie-Man, you'd prefer to be called. Well, dwarf, unless you can conjure up a wizard of my power, you'll not bode well finding precious Mardra. And those wizards are hard to come by these days. I do believe that Black Witch did away with most of them around here before her dragon turned on her."

An angry silence fell over the room. A silence so powerful that Byron and Oberyl heard only the ringing in their ears, a side-effect of hearing the sound of steel clanging against steel one too many times.

"Nothing else to say, boys?" laughed Azar.

A shuffling of footsteps sounded from the entrance to the bloody throne room.

"I do believe, Azar," said a familiar voice, "that there is one wizard on this continent whose magic rivals yours."

Byron and Oberyl turned to see who had spoken those words; the strange hooded man had followed them.

"You," scoffed Azar. "I've seen you pull off some mighty impressive feats of wizardry in your time. But returning from the dead, that's a trick I myself don't even know the secret of. Well, happy hunting, boys."

Azar's spectral form vanished from the throne room.

"You again," Byron gasped. "I'm not sure if it's a pleasure or a curse to see you."

The hooded man said nothing, but somehow Byron could tell he was smiling beneath his hood.

"So are you here to help us or not?" asked Byron.

"And what did you do with Lillia?" asked Oberyl.

"Lillia has a part to play in this," said the hooded man. "But she'll do no good following the two of you around, especially to Bathoria."

"Bathoria," gasped Oberyl.

"Yes, Eerie-man," laughed the stranger. "You've been there. I know."

"Once," said Oberyl. "And I'd hoped never to return."

"Few who find themselves in those mountains ever have the luxury of being able to return," said the hooded man. "But you aren't like most others, Oberyl O'Garyn. Lucky for Byron he has such a seasoned traveler as a comrade."

"Lucky indeed," said Byron. "But how do you know we'll find Mardra in Bathoria?"

"That is where Azar and his demon mistress reside," said the hooded man. "And they both draw their dark magic from those cursed mountains. And, I do believe you had a quite time with that demon-girl not long ago in Westmyrh."

"Indeed I did," said Byron over Oberyl's laughter. "How do you know so much, stranger?"

"All that will be revealed in time, barbarian. Now the two of you had better head west, and make haste. But be sure to stop at the Staggering Stallion inn in Bahrmont. It shouldn't be hard to find; it's the filthiest inn in that entire realm. There you will find a wizard named Parryn. Parryn holds the key to Azar's mountain fortress. Best of luck."

"I guess we'll need horses," said Byron.

The hooded man whistled, and into the throne room trotted the same horses Byron and Oberyl had left behind before entering the town square. "I found these two wandering the woods. I believe they should suit you well."

"Thank you," said Byron.

"Don't mention it," replied the hooded man, then vanished in a dramatic cloud of smoke.

"How long do you suppose it'll take us to reach Bahrmont?" asked Byron.

“Four days, if we haul ass,” replied Oberyl.

*

In his underground lair beneath the mountains of Bathoria, Azar sat quiet and content on his throne made of human bones. To his left stood his prized, shapeshifting demoness. Chained around the neck and nude, Mardra, Leigh and Lynette sat on display. Only dark magic could strip them of their pride, for all the combat skill in the world could not help them against a binding spell.

Standing before the throne stood three misfits who had the reputations of brutal, merciless killers.

“One at a time, state your names and credentials,” said Azar.

“I am Darrin Gralwort,” said the first, a massive hulk of a man with scars about his arms and face, and a patch covering one eye. “I’ve got three barbarian slayings to my credit. I’ve killed men, women and children. I do not discriminate. Nor do I fail. When there is coin offered, I kill. When there is excessive coin offered, I elaborate in any way the buyer requests.”

“Very good,” said Azar, and pointed to the man next to Darrin Gralwort. “And you?”

“I am Erico Tanzin,” said the man, shorter and thinner than Gralwort, but finely chiseled with a face meaner than a murdloch. “I may not have slain any barbarians, yet. But, I served on the frontlines in the wars of Atythea. My kill count was the highest among my army. I turned down all offers of promotion and advancement in favor of hired kills. Much like the man next to me, I have yet to fail in bringing back the head or whatever body parts are desired of my targets."

"Splendid," said Azar, and pointed to the last man. "And lastly, you?"

"You may call me Tim," he said. He stood shirtless, wearing only leather pants and boots. Strapped across his chest was a bandolier with numerous knives and blades attached. "My combat skills are good enough, but I seldom have the need to test them. I am the best blade thrower on this entire continent."

In a flash he swiped a blade from his bandolier. A split second later Azar heard the agonized cries of a pig-faced goblin. All heads in the stony throne room turned to find one of Azar's many goblin guards with a knife handle sticking out from its eye socket. The goblin breathed its last breath and slumped to the ground.

"Impressive," said Azar. "It seems the three of you are well versed in the art of killing. But how good are you all in the art of capture?"

"Flawless," said Darrin Gralwort. "It's simple, really. You just subdue your target to the point of killing, but bind them at the wrists instead of plunging a blade through their throat."

The other two outlaws nodded their agreement.

"Very well then," said Azar. "Your targets are a barbarian and a dwarf. A duo like that should be rather easy to spot. They are travelling here by horseback from Rosecrown. I would like for you to head them off in Zarn. I estimate they will arrive there by in two days' time. I urge you not to kill them, though you may hurt them all you like. Bring them to me alive, and your reward will earn you all an early retirement."

"Byron will turn the three of you inside out," laughed Mardra. "And lay your guts to rest in a tomb built of your own bones."

A knife landed in the stone ground less than an inch from Mardra's leg.

"Care to place a bet on that, girl?" asked Tim the bladesman.

"My only hope is that Byron drags the three of you back here alive so the girls and I can assist in your slaughter."

"That will be quite enough, Mardra dear," said Azar. "Gentleman, be off. Ride like the wind until you find your targets. Precious coin awaits you when you return."

"A question, if I may," said Tim.

"Certainly," Azar replied.

"If they're on their way here, why not just let them come?"

Azar snapped his fingers, and Tim fell dead on the stone floor.

"I need you to intercept them," Azar said to the remaining two outlaws. "My reason is of no importance to you. Now go."

*

After two days and nights of near nonstop riding, Byron finally conceded to Oberyl's request for food and a night's rest.

"Fine," grunted Byron. "I suppose it will only do us good. Even in my desperation to free Mardra, I find myself growing tired. I'll do Mardra no good showing up with the energy and alertness of a zombie."

"Thank you," said Oberyl with a heavy sigh. "We have just crossed into the territory of Zarn. At the first inn we spot we shall tie up the horses and eat. I promise I'll be ready to ride out after but a few hours of comfortable sleep."

For less than an hour the duo rode on until they found the town square. The town itself was filthy and rundown, as were every house and building they passed. Finally, they came upon an inn with no name or sign posted out front, but the smell of spilt ale and pipe smoke bid them welcome.

"Looks like as good an inn as any we'll find here," said Byron.

"Then let's tie up these horses and get ourselves some beef and taters," said Oberyl. "And if the whores are as skanky as this town is, I think I'll buy myself a bit of fun while we're here."

"You said you'd be rested and ready to set out in the morning," Byron reminded him.

"And what better a thing to put me to sleep than a good romp with a professional?"

"Whatever suits you," groaned Byron.

In a dark alley beside the inn there was a tying post where several horses awaited their masters. After tying their horses up they went into the inn to find a tavern room full of the dregs of Zarn.

"You sure about picking up a whore in this place?"

Byron asked Oberyl.

“I’ve done worse,” Oberyl replied, looking around. In the corner two men were trading fists while an unfortunate looking woman with more gaps in her mouth than teeth watched on. After one man produced a dagger from his belt and slit the other’s throat, the woman took him by the arm and led up up the stairs in the the back of the tavern. “But, I suppose it won’t be the end of the world if I have to wank myself to sleep tonight.”

“Are you two looking for food and lodging?” asked a rotund man whose belly hung exposed from below his ill fitting shirt.

“We are,” said Byron. “Are you the innkeeper? And how much?”

“I am,” said the fat innkeeper. “And we don’t take kindly to outsiders around here. That’ll be fifty silver pieces for each of you.”

“Fifty silver pieces!” hooted Oberyl. “We could almost buy our own inn for that!”

“Well unless the two of you are bards or jugglers or willing to provide some kind of entertainment to keep these people here and buying ale, I see the two of you turning around and finding food and lodging elsewhere.”

“Very well then,” said Byron.

“Arsehole,” muttered Oberyl as they turned to exit the inn.

“Some hospitality,” groaned Byron once they reached the alley to untie their horses. After mounting and adjusting their saddles they were approached by two motley looking fellows.

"Nice horses," said one of them, a brutish mass of scars and muscle with a patch over one eye. "They for sale?"

"Not tonight," said Byron. "We're leaving, good sirs."

"Oh, why not stay a bit," said the man. "Hop on down and let's chat."

Oberyl, already pissed off at being denied food and a bed, took his feet out of the stirrups and made to jump down and crush some skulls.

"Do you need some help getting down?" the other man said to Oberyl as he struggled with the saddle.

"I can dismount a horse just fine," Oberyl scoffed back, and slid down off his horse. "And I think the two of you picked the wrong night to cross a barbarian and an Eerie-man."

"Well," began the man with the eye patch, "no need to get angry. But if you've got any sentimental attachment to these animals, I suggest you say your goodbyes now."

"For horse thieves, the two of you aren't very clever," said Byron, tensing his hands into fists.

"Oh, we're not here for the horses. It's the two of you we've come to fetch."

"Now I think the two of you must be plain stupid," laughed Oberyl.

"Think again," said the leaner man, pulling a long shiny blade out from his belt. "Now let's do this our way and things will go nice and easy."

Oberyl slid down on the ground between the man's legs and thrust his fist upward into his balls. As the man hooted and howled in agony Oberyl sprung back up onto his feet and threw the man out into the center of the road.

Byron had already planted his knee into the gut of the bigger man and thrown him out into the road as well, where an excited group of spectators were gathering around to watch the fight.

"Now, explain yourselves," said Byron as he and Oberyl strutted out into the road with axe and hammer drawn. "You do this *our way* and things will go easy for the two of you."

"We were instructed not to kill you," said the big man. "Please don't make us disobey orders."

Both men drew swords from scabbards that hung from their backs.

"Did you hear that, Oberyl?" laughed Byron. "They're asking us to cooperate."

"Seems a fairly reasonable request," Oberyl scoffed back. "Except they don't seem to know quite who they're dealing with."

"I won't be too sad if I lose out on a hefty payment," began the smaller, leaner man, "if it means I get to go down in history as the one who laid Byron the Usurper to waste."

"For the last time, I am not a fucking usurper!" howled Byron. "Regicide, yes. Usurper, no. Now, how many pieces would you like me to cut you up into?"

"And just how flat would you like your skull to be?" Oberyl said to the bigger man.

"No one cares about you, dwarf," the big man replied. "I'll kill you for fun, sure. But don't be jealous of your friend just because it's his head the continent wants a platter."

"Don't you two think it's a good time to walk away and rethink your lives?" asked Byron. "No one has yet succeeded in killing or even really causing me harm. And plenty fiercer than the two of you have tried."

The duo of outlaws responded by swinging their swords high and low, only to be parried by their targets. More and more people began gathering around to watch on as the deadly fight was set into action.

"I'll still give you guys a chance to walk away from this," said Byron, dancing casually around sword swings. "You must know by now you've gotten yourself way in over your heads."

"You will surrender and you will be dragged back to Bathoria with us," said the big man.

"We're headed there anyways," said Byron, deflecting the big man's blade with his axe. "Why the hells would Azar send these two clowns to make sure we get there?"

"He must want to keep us from getting the key," said Oberyl.

"So I guess he's probably watching this right now and knows our every move," said Byron.

"Well then I say we give him a real good show," Oberyl shot back, and sent his hammer plunging down into the knee cap of the smaller man.

"I agree!" Byron grabbed the big man's sword hand and squeezed, breaking the hand and crunching the fingers. After knocking him down to the ground with the butt of his axe handle he added, "How exactly should we make this an entertaining display for Azar?"

"I've got an idea," said Oberyl, planting his boot firmly down on the throat of the smaller man. "It all depends on how kinky you're feeling."

"Oberyl my friend, I'm feeling *very* kinky all of a sudden."

Oberyl turned the smaller man over and propped him up on his knees. He reached around and unbuckled the man's pants, pulling them down around the knees.

"I'm not gonna fuck him!" laughed Byron.

"Nor am I," Oberyl snickered back. "But his big friend there is going to get a nice close viewing of the last thing this guy ate."

"You can't be serious!" Byron gasped.

"Dead serious, Byron. You'd be surprised what the human asrehole is capable of."

Byron dragged the big man over and placed his face firmly between the cheeks of his partner's ass. After a great deal of pushing and maneuvering, the big man's nose was planted firmly in the asshole.

"Now hold him steady," said Oberyl, and began hammering away at the back of the big man's head.

"I don't think it's working," said Byron after the big man's head was flattened against the ass in a sticky, gooey mess.

"Perhaps not," laughed Oberyl, drawing back his hammer. "But I'd say we put on a good show for these people."

"Agreed," said Byron as the entire town square hollered and cheered.

"But we're still without food and beds," said Oberyl.

"Nonsense!" came the voice of the fat innkeeper as he ran out into the road with his belly jiggling all over. "I said you could offer my patrons entertainment in exchange for dinner and rooms, and seeing as my tavern just emptied out to watch this show, I'll make good on my word, even if you are a couple of outsiders. Now let's all get back inside. A round of drinks with the barbarian and the dwarf on me!"

*

For two more days the duo rode, stopping only to eat, sleep and shit. Groggy from days of not bathing, Byron showed little enthusiasm as they entered the village of Bahrmont, which bordered the mountains of Bathoria.

"At long last, we are here, Byron," said Oberyl, not showing much excitement either.

"Now we just need to find the Staggering Stallion," said Byron. "I do hope it's close. And I do hope they've got baths. My taint feels like the tanned hide of a pig, and surely doesn't smell much better."

"I share your pain, friend," said Oberyl. "I look forward to getting some feeling back in my nuts. Hopefully there are some nice wenches to accompany us in the baths that will help with that." Byron gave no reply. "I know. The big bad barbarian has taken a vow of celibacy. I'm dying to lay eyes upon a woman so majestically beautiful she can place a barbarian's cock-and-balls under lock and key."

Byron laughed at that, saying, "You have no idea, little friend. Throughout this whole continent, and I'd wager even the uncharted lands beyond its surrounding ocean, there could not be another like her."

"You should have been a poet," said Oberyl.

"So tell me," began Byron, "what was your experience in Bathoria like? I once did battle with a creature from that land."

"Oh you did?" asked Oberyl. "Tell me of it."

"She was a beautiful woman," said Byron. "Or so I thought. But there was much more to her, such as a serpent that came out of her snatch that damn near strangled me to death."

"Ahh yes," laughed Oberyl. "A snatcher!"

"They're actually called that?"

"Well, it's not their official name, but yes, the common man refers to them as such. And good for you. Few men have lived through encountering one."

"But what of your experiences in Bathoria?" asked Byron.

"Ahh yes," said Oberyl, shifting uncomfortably in his saddle. "Well, it was several decades ago at this point. I was a young adventurer travelling the continent looking for trouble and treasure."

"Did you find any treasure in Bathoria?"

"You could say that. Bathoria is where I found the magic of slow aging and a rather extended life. That's why I look so damn good for a seventy-eight year-old Eerie-man. But that's too long a tale to tell now. I think we are drawing near Bahrmont, and I've got a shit in the chamber that's damn near ready to poke its head out of my arse."

"I find myself in a similar predicament."

"What I will tell you, though," began Oberyl, "is that any lore you may have heard about Bathoria is not only likely true, but tells merely half the terror of what truly resides in those mountains. It is truly a wretched hive of scum and demonry. Have you heard of vampires?"

"Of course," laughed Byron.

"Well, my friend, they are real," said Oberyl.

"I've seen dragons, snatchers and murdlochs. Sea monsters, dirt dwellers and centaurs. I've no reason to think vampires aren't real."

"Good. An open mind will be helpful on this quest. I did battle with and killed several vampires. Much like snatchers and murdlochs, their deadliness lies in that they are often unidentifiable until it's too late. So your vow of chastity will serve you well. Speaking of which, look."

The duo had reached the first signs of civilization; a few whores were standing at the rim of the town square. Byron trotted along undeterred while Oberyl cast each girl a glance, smiling and winking.

Dusk was beginning to settle, and several merchants were packing up their wares and wheeling them off on carts to make room for the nighttime street entertainment. Jugglers, mimes and magicians were beginning to unpack their tools of the trade where fruit and vegetable mongers had just vacated.

"Might you know where we can find an inn called The Staggering Stallion?" Byron asked a girl passing by who was pushing a cart full of vegetables.

The girl stopped, looked up and pulled down the bodice of her dirty dress, revealing an ample, creamy set of breasts.

"Well, dear," said Byron, "that was not quite the response I had anticipated."

"I do know where you can find The Staggering Stallion, sir," she said. "But if you're looking for a whore, I can offer you my services. Every bit as good as the girls at the Stallion, and at surely half the cost." The girl picked up a large cucumber from her cart and proceeded to make it disappear down her throat, then slowly pulled it out showing absolutely no signs of gagging or loss of breath. "It's been a tough year for the harvest, you know. A girl must use all of her talents to get by these days."

Byron tossed the girl a couple of coins from his pocket. "That won't be necessary girl. Consider this a payment for allowing me to lay eyes upon your gorgeous tits and for whatever helpful information you can give me regarding where we might find The Staggering Stallion. We've ridden for days, and are looking only for food and rest."

The girl pointed behind her, where a row of buildings extended down the busy road. "Right there," she said.

Byron and Oberyl looked, groaning upon the realization that the sign for The Staggering Stallion was not but thirty feet from where their horses stood.

"Thanks for the coins!" laughed the girl, and hurried along with her cart of vegetables.

"A cunning one," said Byron, trotting his horse along to a tying post on the side of the road.

"Cunning you say?" scoffed Oberyl. "That's not

cunning. That's cunting. The girl was just less of a damn fool than the two of us. Can't blame her, though. Bathoria is like an infected land, its infection stretches out beyond and taints the land and the people for as far as it can reach. That girl would likely do a lot worse than take our money to survive."

"She wasn't all bad," said Byron. "She at least let us see her tits. And I was both impressed and entertained by what she did with that cucumber. She gave me something for my money."

"I can't disagree with you there," laughed Oberyl. "But we must be cautious. The closer you get to Bathoria, the more dangerous people get. Just remember your vow and try not to get lost staring at too many other tits or you'll find yourself face to face with a snatcher again."

After tying their horses and stretching their legs, they slowly approached The Staggering Stallion.

"Okay," said Byron. "This should be easy. We go in, we find a privy to void our bowels, we find this wizard, and we go get the key to Azar's lair."

"Sounds easy enough," said Oberyl.

Byron pushed the doors of the inn open, and stopped dead in his tracks as an entire tavern full of old, bearded and cloaked men looked up at them.

"Great," groaned Byron. "It's a wizard bar."

"I should have expected yet another obstacle," said Oberyl.

Byron glanced around and found a few empty seats right up at the bar where a dashing and buxom lady was serving drinks and making small talk with a few drunken wizards.

"Well, Oberyl, let's find that privy, then we'll go sit down and have a drink. And start asking questions."

*

After a good and thorough sit on the privy for both parties, Byron and Oberyl sauntered back into the tavern portion of the inn and took a seat at the bar. The bar wench was a young, gorgeous thing, pale of skin with dark ebony hair and bright green eyes. And of course, her most delightful assets: her large and exposed breasts, were fully on display.

"How may I help you boys?" she asked in a brogue similar to Oberyl's. "You two look like the ale drinking type." The girl looked over at Oberyl. "Especially you, cutie."

"Correct, my dear," said Oberyl.

"Two big ales," said Byron. "And we'd love to see a food menu."

"We've got roasted mutton and mashed potatoes," said the girl. "That's about it today."

"Two plates of that as well, please," said Byron as Oberyl nodded in agreement.

The girl poured their ales, then took off to put in their food order.

"Lovely girl," said Byron.

"Especially those eyes," added Oberyl. "They remind me of the emerald grass back in the Eerie."

"Perhaps you should have been a poet as well, friend," laughed Byron. "Maybe once this quest is over and I've gotten Mardra back you and I will hang up these weapons and become bards. It's a much safer occupation."

"But the payoff would be minimal," said Oberyl. "You ever see a bard save a poor damsel in distress, granting him the reward of spilling his nuts out onto her smiling face?"

"Can't say that I have," Byron admitted.

"Then I think the danger we place ourselves in is well worth it," said Oberyl. "Now, let's get to figuring out how we're going to locate this Parryn fellow."

"Why not just ask?" said Byron. "The girl seems nice enough. Hells, she even shows her tits like that last girl."

"We must practice the art of subtlety," said Oberyl. "Two strangers showing up in a bar full of wizards, which we are not, and asking for someone by name is not the best idea."

The duo looked around the tavern; in a room full of wizards it was difficult to spot one who stood out from the others. Wizards were all unique, and highly eccentric in their choices of garb. With the added distraction of the nearly nude serving girls parading around in nothing but thongs and necklaces, scanning the room seemed to be a moot point.

The green-eyed bar wench returned with their food, and the duo immediately started gorging.

"What brings you two warriors to this here wizard bar?" she asked. "It's nice to see a little exposed muscle instead of saggy cloaks and scraggly beards, I must say."

"We're, uhh, vacationing," said Byron.

"The two of you together?" asked the girl.

"Yes," Byron replied.

"I see," said the girl with a puzzled look. "Queers?"

"No, no, dear," laughed Byron. "Not that there's anything wrong with that, of course. Just a couple of friends."

Byron realized how awful he was at lying as Oberyl shook his head in embarrassment.

"So the two of you, armed with axe and hammer, are just two buddies on a little getaway from the stress of the working life," said the girl. "Sounds highly believable. Why not tell me what you're really doing here, boys."

"We're searching for someone," said Byron. "Someone we believe can help us."

"And who might this someone be?" the girl asked. "Do they have a name?"

"Parryn," said Oberyl. "He's a wizard. Heard of him?"

"Indeed I have," the girl replied with a serious, unreadable look upon her face. "It's been a long time since anyone came around here looking for him."

"Might you know if he's here?" asked Byron. "We would very much like to speak with him."

"He's here all right. Would you like me to take you to him?"

"That would be great," said Byron. "Please and thank you."

The girl reached out over the bar and placed each of her hands on Byron and Oberyl's foreheads. As she pulled her hands back the duo felt as if they'd been walloped over the head by maces. Before them, where the lovely girl had been standing behind the bar, a monster of hideous design now stood with ashy, cracked skin and eyes yellower than hay. The room had gone black and cloudy like the landscape of a nightmare. Where a moment ago they had been in a tavern full of wizards, they were now surrounded by monsters just like the one in front of them.

"What kind of foul magic is this?" cried Byron, reaching back for his axe.

A lightning bolt shot out from nowhere, knocking his axe to the ground. Oberyl's hammer fell down next to it only a second later.

"State your true business here," gurgled the monster.

"We are in search of a wizard named Parryn," said Byron. "I told you true."

"What need have you of Parryn?" the monster asked.

"We were told Parryn held a very important key," said Byron. "A key that will gain us access to the fortress of an evil wizard named Azar."

With the mention of Azar's name came thunder booming from up above. The entire tavern disappeared; above them now was a black void of a sky with winged demons swirling about, screeching and howling.

The monster touched their foreheads again, and suddenly all had returned to the way it was only moments ago. The roof was back up over their heads, and once again there were drunken wizards all around them sitting at their tables and minding their own affairs.

"Something wrong, boys?" the once again lovely girl asked.

"I think I just had a terrible hallucination," said Byron, reaching back to find his axe was once again sheathed at his back.

"Same here," said Oberyl.

"You did," said the girl with a laugh. "I was just testing you."

"Testing us?" asked Byron. "Why?"

"To see what your business here truly was," said the girl. "Now tell me, who told you about the key? There was only one person who could know that, and, well, for him to have told you I hold the key would be impossible."

"We don't really know who it was," said Byron. "He didn't reveal his identity. Secretive fellow. Always wearing a hood that covers his face."

"When did he tell you?"

"Only four days ago," said Byron.

"Wait, wait," said Oberyl. "You just said that *you* hold the key."

"Shit," muttered the girl. "I did, didn't I?"

"So, you are Parryn?" asked Byron.

"Indeed," scoffed the girl. "I had hoped to keep that secret from you a while longer, but I guess I blew that. Typical, though, that a couple of oafs like yourselves would assume that an all powerful wizard had to be a man."

"Well, I always thought that a female wizard would be referred to as a sorceress," said Byron.

"Get with the times, you ogre," hissed Parryn. "People of magic no longer care for gender labels."

"Of course," said Byron. "My apologies. So how would we go about getting this key from you?"

Parryn turned around and bent down under the bar, giving Byron and Oberyl a much appreciated shot of her thong clad rear. As she stood up she placed a small, copper key down between their plates.

"That was easy," said Byron.

"I had imagined the key to an evil, forbidden fortress would look a little more…impressive," said Oberyl.

"This key, you buffoons, is the key to a room upstairs with a moon and star carved on the door. Finish your meals and wait for me there. You can also feel free to wash up. If I'm to ride out to Bathoria with the two of you, I'd prefer you not smelling like horse shit."

*

Byron walked out of the bath clean, shaven and feeling anew. Oberyl, who had bathed before him, sat on his bed polishing the steel of his hammer. Byron stretched and sighed, shaking the tension out of his taut muscles.

"You seem to have taken on a more cavalier attitude all of a sudden," said Oberyl. "What's the deal?"

"We are close now," Byron replied. "Mardra is close. I can sense it."

"Well, I suppose a little optimism never hurt anyone. However, I don't think you're quite ready for what we'll find when we enter into those mountains."

"Oberyl, friend, I'm ready for anything. Vampires, demons, snatchers, you name it. Bring it on, I say."

"I like your attitude," said Oberyl. "But please, for the love of the nine gods, put some fucking pants on. I've no interest in seeing your pecker."

A knock sounded on the door, and in walked Parryn. She

too appeared to have bathed, and was now wearing a flowing white dress that clung just right to the curves of her body that before had been revealed.

"Well hello there," she said, looking down at Byron's exposed cock. "You two are awfully comfortable around each other in close quarters. Am I still to believe the two of you are merely friends?"

"Believe what you will," said Byron. "We've got important business ahead of us. You can believe that Oberyl and I are lovers for all it matters to me."

"Then get dressed and go to your horses," said Parryn. "We must ride out tonight, at once."

"In the dead of night?" asked Oberyl.

"Are you scared?" asked Parryn.

"Well, certainly not," the Eerie-man replied in a huff. "I've been to Bathoria before. Nighttime seems hardly the right time to make such a trip."

"Don't listen to my little friend," said Byron. "This quest is not as important to him as it is to me."

"And what is this quest of yours exactly, barbarian?" asked Parryn. "What could be so important to draw you into the mountain lair of… That reminds me. That evil wizard you seek, his name is not to be uttered. He has ears everywhere."

"He knows we're coming," said Byron. "And with magic as powerful as his, I'm sure he's watching us from his lair as we speak."

"You're wiser than I thought," Parryn said with a snicker. "Lucky for you two I have cloaking magic that can hide us. But please, do not say his name."

"Fair enough," Byron agreed.

"So now tell me, why should I, a complete stranger to the two of you, venture out on this damn fool journey? Why should I help you?"

"I don't know what I can say to convince you, dear Parryn," said Byron. "But Az…the one whose name we shall not mention has taken someone very dear to me. I know not how I could repay you for accompanying us on this venture, but I assure you that I will, one way or another."

"You give me no good reason to come along," laughed Parryn. "Repayment of debts is meaningless to me. I do just fine running this establishment, tending bar for drunken wizards and serving as den mother to the finest whores in the realm. But, I've heard about you, *Byron*. And I believe there is something special about you. You are no ordinary barbarian. I believe that somehow, some way, you are capable of bringing an end to the evil of that black wizard and his demon whore. And with me assisting you, it just might be a sure thing. We will find your precious Mardra."

"So then you do know what our quest is," said Byron.

"A wise wizard knows more than they let on," said Parryn.

"Well thank you for the kind words," said Byron, blushing about the cheeks.

"And you," said Parryn, looking down at the bed where Oberyl sat with his hammer. "You best believe I know who you are too. Legend of the dwarf warrior is rich around these parts."

Oberyl growled at the mention of the dwarf word.

"I'm not a—"

"Yes, you're not a dwarf, Oberyl O'Garyn of the Eerie," said Parryn. "My apologies. But believe me when I tell you that the tales I've heard of the dwarf warrior do not paint you in a negative way. How could they, as they paint you as the only warrior known on this continent to have ventured into Bathoria and returned to tell the tale?"

"I guess I can live with that," said Oberyl, smiling as he returned to shining his hammer.

"As Oberyl can probably tell you, the road that passes through those mountains will be littered with the bones of fallen warriors of recent times and centuries past. Though I can cloak us from the eyes of the black wizard, he knows you are coming, and there will be many traps and the nine gods know what else waiting for us all along the way."

"I'm ready for anything," said Byron.

"Well then please put some goddamn pants on and let's be on our way," said Parryn. "I'll meet you out front where your horses are tied."

FOUR

Within two hours of setting out from The Staggering Stallion, Parryn had led Byron and Oberyl by torchlight to where the mountains of Bathoria began. The ride had been mostly silent aside from the unsettling sounds of the Bathorian night and the crackling of torch flame. Byron cared only for finding Mardra, placing his focus on what perils may wait ahead. Oberyl's silence, despite adamant denial, was a result of his mind's unease about returning to the cursed place.

The closer they got to the mountains the darker the night became. Luckily, Parryn employed her magic to keep the torches lit without fear of burning out. Byron silently prayed to the nine that her sorcery stretched beyond the ability to perform mere parlor tricks.

The ground beneath them had gradually gone from green and full of life to black and dead. With the mountains now in sight, not a plant, blade of grass or living tree was to be found.

Parryn brought her mare to a stop as their path narrowed

to a thin strip of ash and rubble. They were now at the very foot of the Bathorian mountains, and could no longer see the high peaks above. Overhead they could only see the hanging branches of the dead, brittle trees, and hints of the mountain that showed through the holes in the canopy. Unlike the ground beneath their horses' feet, the massive mountain had a brilliant purple sheen to it, as if the rock itself was alive and flowing with evil. Oberyl listened closely, and through the night's silence and the crackling torches he felt as if he could hear creeping whispers resonate from within the mountain.

Oberyl cleared his throat and spoke. "If we return from this quest, Byron, you fucking owe me, bub."

"Oberyl, my dear friend," said Byron, "if we return from this quest I will either have the one and only thing that matters to me in this world, or nothing at all. I would have to pledge myself to *your* service, for I'd have nothing else to give."

"I'd at least settle for a handjob," grunted Oberyl. Both Byron and Parryn turned their gaze to Oberyl and raised an eyebrow. "Enough of your sappy bullshit, Byron. Before we set out to this mountain you were all balls and cock. Now we're here and suddenly you're a blubbering pussy again. We're here, we're going to rescue your girl, and we're going to leave this fucking place better than we were when we came to it. But if you don't stop whining I'll shove this here dwarf cock up your arse and show your dear Mardra just what a barbarian you truly are. Now chin up, and let's fucking do this!"

"I do think I like you very much, Eerie-man!" howled

Parryn, emitting a thunderous laugh as she jumped off her mare gracefully, landing square on her sleek leather boots. Oberyl couldn't help but notice the way her shiny white dress blew up in the air as she dismounted, flashing him the lovely sight of her barely concealed lady parts. "From here we must venture on foot," she said. "No horse can handle the terrain ahead. Nor would they try."

"Can't you use magic on the horses?" asked Byron. "Maybe coax them along a bit."

Parryn laughed again, saying, "Horses are wiser than us humans, and far more stubborn. So stubborn in fact, that they seem to be immune to the magic of people."

Byron and Oberyl dismounted and watched as the three horses galloped free back to Bahrmont.

Parryn lifted her torch and proceeded onto the path that led into darkness.

"Don't hold your torches too high, boys," she said. "The dead wood overhead will catch flame fast if lit."

Byron and Oberyl looked up and saw how low the branches of the dead trees that lined the path hung; the branches seemed to weave together in a macabre tapestry too intricate to be simply the work of nature. They lifted their torches and hurried along to catch up with Parryn.

"So you remembered to bring that key along, right?" asked Byron.

"It would be hard for me to forget," said Parryn. "The key is a spell. And I am the only one who knows it, or so I thought… which raises the question of just who this strange hooded man was who told you about it."

"How did you come to know the spell?" asked Byron.

"A wizard told me," said Parryn. "The wizard who created it."

"Well, I'd say there's a good chance then that this wizard and the hooded man are the same guy," said Oberyl.

"That would be the easy answer," said Parryn. "Except for the fact that the wizard who taught me the spell is dead."

Byron thought that over as the trio hiked along over the rocky, uneven path.

"Could it be?" he said aloud.

"Could what be?" asked Oberyl.

"Nothing, I suppose," said Byron. "It's just that when the hooded man appeared in Rosecrown, the black wizard made mention of him having returned from the dead. Not important at the moment, though. Best we just focus on the here and now."

As Byron finished his last words rocks came tumbling down the mountains around them. Parryn simply raised her free hand and commanded the falling boulders to stillness, locking them in place where they had stopped.

"Neat trick," said Byron, taking comfort in Parryn's apparent strength in sorcery. "I'm starting to see how so few people have ever returned from this place."

"We've barely gone past the border of Bathoria," laughed Parryn. "But now we know that despite my cloaking magic, the black wizard knows we are here."

"How can he know if he can't see us?" asked Oberyl.

"Don't waste time trying to make sense of magic," said Parryn. "Especially Azar's… Shit, remind me not to say his name again."

A bolt of lightning shot down before them, accompanied by a booming clap of thunder. Where the lightning had struck appeared a ghostly woman with chains bound around her feet and arms.

"Gods!" cried Byron. "Mardra!"

"Byron!" cried the ghost. "Please don't bother. Turn around while you can. I'm already dead!"

"It's not really her ghost, Byron," said Parryn. "Surely you're smarter than to fall for such a cheap trick. Stay back."

Byron approached the ghost undeterred, hearing not a word of Parryn's warning.

"Mardra… I failed you!" gasped Byron.

"Is he always this fucking stupid?" Parryn asked, looking back at Oberyl.

"Not usually," replied Oberyl. "But certainly always when it comes to Mardra."

Byron fell to his knees, looking up at the ghost.

"Forgive me!" Byron pled to the apparition.

"Byron!" Parryn shouted. "Get back—"

The apparition suddenly morphed into a winged demon, uttering a deafening screech. Byron knew this demon well, and had also seen her take on the corporeal form of Mardra during the incident at Westmyrh.

Byron jumped to his feet and drew his axe with his free hand, using the other to ward the demon away with his torch.

"Be still!" shouted Parryn, raising her free hand in the demon's direction. She uttered a quick spell in an unknown tongue and vanquished the demon into an explosive cloud of red smoke and ash.

"Gods," gasped Byron, wiping away the demon's powdery remains from his face.

"Please listen to me, you fool," muttered Parryn. "Think with your head, not with your heart. You truly are the biggest pussy of a barbarian I've ever met. Though I must admit it's more than a bit charming, put that shit away for the time being and be a fucking barbarian! And furthermore, when I tell you not to go near something, please don't!"

"Right," Byron agreed. "I won't make that mistake again. It's just that the sight of Mardra…"

"Yes, I get it," said Parryn. "You've got a heart bigger than that bulge in your pants. Now keep that axe at the ready and let's continue on."

On they went, ready for another trap or obstacle to show itself at any moment. Hints of laughter sounded out intermittently, echoing around the mountain's crevices; shadows of human form flew by their eyes and disappeared into the darkness.

"Ignore anything you see or hear that isn't a solid physical body," said Parryn. "He is merely trying to raise our anxiety. These shadows and sounds are mere trinkets of dark magic. They will not harm you, but will make you harm yourself if you let them fool you."

Byron nodded his acknowledgment and followed along with his axe held at the ready. A hundred or so yards further into the mountain, he felt a tap at his shoulder.

"Yes, Oberyl," he said.

"I didn't say anything," replied Oberyl.

"I know, but you just tapped me on the..." Byron felt another tap and craned his neck back to look at his shoulder where he saw two heavy drops of thick, congealed blood. Looking up, he gasped.

"Take cover!" cried Oberyl, jumping off to the side of the path pressing his back against the mountain.

Byron and Parryn followed along, cringing at the sight they saw above them.

A massive bat, easily the size of a man, swooped down dripping blood from its mouth. The creature landed on its human-like legs and barred their way.

"You shall not pass," gurgled the bat-monster in a phlegm-and-blood coated growl.

Byron responded with laughter, and said, "Hey, Oberyl. Did you ever notice that bats have cocks and balls just like people?"

"Not until now," replied Oberyl. "Look at that thing. It's tiny!"

Even Parryn joined in on the laughter and said, "No kidding. Is it cold out here or something?"

The bat grimaced, but then snarled its fangs and raised its wings.

"It's cute almost," said Byron with a snicker. "I almost want to go over there and tickle those little balls."

"Ooh, me first!" hooted Oberyl.

"Enough!" hissed the bat-monster. "When I take on my human form it's much bigger. I swear!"

"Oh yeah, let's see it!" said Byron.

"Yeah, show us," added Parryn. "I'll believe that when I

see it."

"Fine!" gurgled the bat, then began slowly morphing into human form. "You see!" it said as it took on the shape of a young, pale man.

"Bigger, sure," said Oberyl. "But still, I'd hardly call that a dick. I'm not even five feet tall and I've got you beat by several measures."

"Is that so, Oberyl?" asked Parryn, looking over to the Eerie-man and widening her eyes.

"Indeed it is," said Oberyl.

"I can vouch for him," said Byron. "As unfortunate as it may be, I've seen the little guy's cock."

"Under what circumstances might that have happened?" asked Parryn.

"Our last quest, when we were travelling to Mount Valgorn," said Byron. "We had a lovely older gal named Phadriel with us. I had the *pleasure* of walking in on Oberyl here ramming her from behind."

Parryn smiled at Oberyl and winked.

"Umm, hello!" cried the man-bat. "I'm supposed to drain the three of you of your blood and bring it back to Azar so he can clone evil replicants of you, and you're not even paying attention to me!"

"How would you do that, exactly?" asked Byron.

"Good question," Oberyl added. "If you're to drink our blood, how would you give it to him? Would you spit it into his mouth like a mother feeding a baby bird?"

"Or would you kiss it into his mouth?" asked Parryn. "Some of my whores back at the inn get requests to kiss a man's seed into their mouths after they suck them off. I could totally picture you and the black wizard doing that. How cute!"

"Isn't there a name for that?" asked Byron.

"A name for what?" asked Parryn.

"What you just said. When a girl spits a man's nut into his mouth."

"I believe that's called a snowball," said Oberyl. "Or at least that's what I've heard it referred to as in all my travels."

"Quiet!" cried the man-bat, and began to reassume his bat form, only to fall back and shrivel as Byron's axe flung and landed in the dead center of his chest.

"That was a good bit of fun," said Byron as he dislodged his axe from the late bat-monster's withered, wrinkly chest. "I suddenly feel like myself again. How much farther to the lair?"

"I believe it is about a mile in from here," said Parryn.

The group travelled on in silence for what seemed to be countless miles, though Parryn showed no sign of worry. Several times Byron believed they had gone around in circles.

"Does it seem to anyone else that we're getting nowhere?" he asked. "And that we've been wandering for a very long time?"

"To you and Oberyl it would seem that way," said Parryn. "Just another trick of the black wizard. He surely realized that his cheap monsters and demons are no real match for us, and is now employing a more invisible form of magic. This is not good, for it means that his magic has gotten into your heads. Worry not, for I am countering that magic with my own. I know exactly where we're going. Just follow me and we'll get there."

The trio continued on but stopped as Oberyl suddenly gasped and slumped down to the ground.

"Oberyl, are you all right?" asked Byron.

"Must have tripped on a rock," replied the Eerie-man. "Just fine."

As Oberyl tried to get back on his feet he realized he could not, and that something had latched on to his leg.

"What the…" he groaned as he looked down and found a skeletal hand reaching up from the ground. With a quick swing of his hammer he shattered the hand, but did not cease the rising of the body attached to it.

The path began to quake and tremble, causing the trio to seek steady ground on the rising rocks off to the side of the path. One after another, bony hands reached up from the ground, then heads, then torsos.

"I think we should be able to make quick work of these things," said Byron. "Assuming there aren't too many."

Faced with about thirty walking corpses, Byron and Oberyl jumped down from the rocks and began demolishing the skeletons which served as more of a hindrance than a threat.

Once the ground was littered with a scattering of bones, and no more skeletons barred their way, Byron grumbled, "Is he going to throw something actually dangerous or scary at us?"

"You may regret those words," said Parryn.

Parryn waited for a reply from Byron but heard instead a grunt and a gasp. She turned to find only Oberyl standing behind her, staring down at the ground where Byron's torch lay, still burning.

"Byron!" screamed Oberyl.

"Where did he go?"

"He was just here a second ago and suddenly he—"

Parryn cried out as she saw Oberyl disappear into a hole that had suddenly opened beneath his feet. She had no hard time figuring out what was likely to happen next, and stood still for a moment rather than delay the inevitable.

*

Byron awoke to the smell of must and mold. As his vision reached clarity he found himself on the floor of a small stone cell barred by a heavy wrought iron gate. He stood up and prepared to pry the bars open by hand, only to discover that his hands were bound by glowing, transparent bonds of a magical design.

"Open the cell!" he cried. "Whatever you want of me, come and get it, Azar you one-eyed fuck-face!"

A duo of pig-faced goblins appeared at the cell door and keyed it open. Each of them grabbed Byron by an arm and led him out. They travelled down a dark and dank corridor lined with prison cells which Byron noticed housed only the badly decomposed and skeletal remains of prisoners past. Byron chose to keep quiet, as he highly doubted he'd get or comprehend any answers from a duo of mindless pig-faces.

At the end of the corridor they came to a massive open

room inhabited by heavily armed goblins. After being dragged through the mob Byron discovered that he was now in the very throne room of Azar, possibly miles below the mountain.

"Where is she!" cried Byron as he saw the grizzly sight of Azar seated upon a throne made entirely of what appeared to be human bones. Before the wizard's feet sitting helpless on the ground, nude but for the iron brace around her neck and the chain that connected it to the floor, was Parryn.

"Why, she's right over there, Byron," hissed Azar, pointing to Byron's left. "And a mighty fine decoration she and the other two are making."

Byron turned as a horde of goblins moved aside revealing Mardra, Leigh and Lynette, nude and gagged, suspended by rope.

"Mardra!" cried Byron. The sight of her, her actual physical body, after so long brought him to the point of choking back a tear or two. But, even Byron knew this was not the time for that, and he drew a casual smile upon his face. "Rest easy, Mardra. You too, Leigh and Lynette. And it's mighty nice to see the two of you again. You won't be hanging up there for much longer."

Their arms were tied at the wrists, drawn out to the sides, stretching as far as they could. Their legs were tied and stretched at the ankles in the same fashion. Positioned perfectly under the center of each of their bodies were long, sharp spikes that, should Mardra or the girls be lowered, would impale them through the womb.

"What is it you want from me?" asked Byron, turning

back to face Azar. "I want only the release of these three girls. Name your price."

"What I want, barbarian, is a life," said Azar. "And I'm only asking for one. If you think about it, one life in exchange for three is a rather good deal. Few evil, dark wizards would be so generous. You see, your bitch-wizard friend here killed my prize."

"Your prize?" asked Byron.

"Yes, you met her back in Westmyrh. Fucked her even. She drained your balls so dry you shriveled up like a—"

"Yeah, I remember," said Byron, cutting the wizard off. He couldn't help but cast Mardra a quick glance to see her reaction. "Hard to blame me since she had taken on the form of Mardra. Really, Mardra, I swear. That was the only reason."

Mardra smiled beneath her gag. As Byron hoped and figured, she wasn't the type to really give a shit.

"So Parryn killed your demon bitch? Just like that? Back at the mountain entry?"

"Yes," groaned Azar.

"Well that seemed a rather easy kill for something you covet highly enough to call a prize," snickered Byron.

"Demons can be a valuable terror, barbarian, but can also be easy to kill. Anyhow, back to the matter at hand. As Parryn has taken a life from me, I demand one in return."

"You want my life?" asked Byron.

"Perhaps," said Azar. "Either yours or your little friend's."

Through the surrounding mob of goblins came two

leading Oberyl out in the same fashion Byron had been.

"You see, Byron," began Azar, "the two of you make a good team. *Too* good a team. One lone dwarf with fighting skills such as little Oberyl has doesn't pose too great a threat to my evil, or the evil of others like me. Nor does one lone barbarian such as yourself. But the two of you breathing the air of this continent together, well, that is just unacceptable. Queen Mirelda and the black witch were good friends of mine, you know."

"So have at us, you cunt!" howled Oberyl.

"Oh no," laughed Azar. "I don't think so." Azar raised a long, bony hand in the air. "Arm them!"

Byron and Oberyl were dragged to the center of the chamber, facing each other. Another pair of goblins came forth and dropped Byron's axe and Oberyl's hammer between them at their feet.

"Ahh yes, my boys," said Azar. "It will be a fight to the death. And you better make it quick too." Azar pointed to where Mardra, Leigh and Lynette were suspended. "For every minute that passes without one of you meeting your makers, the girls will be lowered."

Azar snapped his fingers and the magical bonds that tied the wrists of Byron and Oberyl together vanished. For a little added intimidation, Azar commanded his goblins who were manning the pulleys to lower the girls a few inches each.

"Prepare to die, dwarf," Byron hissed with a cruel scowl drawn upon his face.

Oberyl was at first shocked that Byron seemed to be going along with Azar's deal. After all they'd been through in the short time they'd been together, and with Oberyl's sworn allegiance to the man, it simply couldn't be. But a quick wink of the barbarian's eye put his mind at ease.

Oberyl heard Byron say something, only he did not see the words come from the barbarian's mouth. "We'll figure something out," Byron's voice said.

Oberyl merely thought his next words but heard them aloud as if he had spoken them. "How did you do that?"

"I'm not sure," Byron replied, again without actually speaking.

"Start fighting and make it look as real as possible," said the voice of Parryn. "And do not look over at me! I'm using magic, you fools. Azar doesn't seem to be wise to it, so don't do anything that might tip him off."

Byron and Oberyl reached for their weapons and immediately began thrashing away at each other.

"Beautiful!" howled Azar over the growls and cheers of his goblin army. "Give it all you've got, boys!"

"I'm surprised neither of you thought of this on your own," came the voice of Parryn, "but here is what you must do…"

Byron and Oberyl continued their brutal display of combat, slashing and pounding axe and hammer as Azar cheered on from his throne, and Parryn silently instructed them.

"Hit Byron hard in the stomach," said Parryn's voice.

"Are you nuts?" the Eerie-man thought back.

"If one of you doesn't make contact soon Azar will likely know we've got some trickery afoot."

Just then the ropes holding Mardra, Leigh and Lynette were lowered, dropping their womanhoods a few inches closer to impalement.

Oberyl pulled back and swung his hammer just hard enough into Byron's stomach to make it look convincing; Byron went sprawling back near the spikes above which Mardra and the girls were suspended. As he tried to get to his feet he tripped and went careening into three of the nearest goblins. As they tried to push him back onto the the fighting floor he swung his axe horizontally and, with ease, took off all three snouted goblin heads with one slice.

Byron snatched up and lobbed the goblin heads over to Oberyl who sheathed his hammer and caught each one. As Oberyl planted the helmeted heads on the spikes below the girls, Byron went to work at their restraining ropes with his axe. Oberyl, showing Azar just what a team he and Byron truly made, snatched the swords off the three headless goblin bodies and tossed each one to the girls as they were freed, all in such good time that none of the still living goblin army could reach them.

Byron, Oberyl, and the three nude female warriors went back-to-back in a circle at the center of the chamber while the goblin army surrounded them.

Mardra clutched Byron's arm and jumped up to kiss his cheek.

"I always knew you'd come to your senses and come back to me," she said.

"I suppose I did too," Byron replied. "And now we see the price I pay for waiting as long as I did."

"We'll make up for all that lost time once we get out of here," laughed Mardra.

"I take it you've trained Leigh and Lynette like I told them you would."

"All that and then some, Byron. And from what they tell me, you gave them a little training and then some too." Mardra gave Byron a coy wink. "You dirty boy."

Byron immediately blushed.

"Like I care," said Mardra with a snicker. "Now let's focus."

"Okay, love birds," said Leigh. Or Lynette. Byron wasn't quite sure. "We took on this many goblins back in Rosecrown, and that was without the aid of Byron and his cute little friend."

"Right, sister," said the other twin. "Now let's tear this goblin horde a new set of assholes.

The five warriors slowly dispersed, crushing, slashing and hammering goblin heads with ease. Azar simply sat and watched on as if this all meant nothing to him.

"I do suppose I can hold on to one trophy," he said, pulling on Parryn's leash.

With a mere mental impulse he broke the chain around her neck where it connected to the ground, and vanished with her in a cloud of pink smoke.

"The wizard and Parryn are gone, Byron!" cried Oberyl over the gurgles of two goblins whose heads he had just hammered flat. "What's our next move?"

"Slay the lot of these goblin fucks and get the hells out of here!" Byron hollered back after hacking off the arm of a goblin. "The hooded man led us to Parryn once, I'm sure he'll lead us to her again!"

"Do you know how to get out of here, Byron?" Mardra called out to him, pulling her sword out of the throats of three goblins she had just skewered.

Byron looked over to answer her, trying ever so hard not to get lost in the sight of her graceful body dancing with the sword, and her massive breasts bouncing so plump and bountiful. How he wanted to just drop his axe and run to her ample bosom. "Nope!"

"The girls and I will carve a path through the goblins! You two follow along and guard the rear!"

"And don't get too distracted by the sight of our asses, little man," said one of the twins to Oberyl.

"We know you've been staring," added the other.

*

Azar, along with Parryn, appeared in a puff of smoke just inside the entryway into Bathoria, where the path narrowed between the mountains.

"I hope you're looking forward to a life without magic," he said, dragging her along by the chain that served as a leash. "At least until you are broken in and trained to use magic to do my bidding. I've been long thinking it's time to take on a new personal whore."

"You don't really think you're going to pull that off, do you, Azar?" hissed Parryn. "I'm not some mindless demon skank like your last one. I'm one of the strongest wizards on this continent."

"All in due time, my dear," said Azar. "You'll soon learn to worship me. They always do. Besides, I thrive on a good challenge."

Dawn had broken, and beams of sun shined through the holes in the overhead canopy of dead branches. Azar tugged hard on Parryn's leash and dragged her out onto the dead field. As Azar was about to further degrade his new servant, he gasped and stopped dead in his tracks.

Parryn's laughter sounded high in the fresh morning air. The black wizard, for the first time in a thousand years, had been bested.

"No…" groaned Azar at the obstacle that stood before them.

"Unhand her and surrender," said a voice that Parryn had not heard in several years, a voice she thought belonged to a dead man.

"Somehow I always knew you'd return!" cried Parryn in a fit of joy.

"You may have put my reign to and end," said Azar. "But don't think I didn't set a few traps for your friends back in the mountain."

Azar snapped his fingers.

*

Mardra and the twins had successfully led Byron and Oberyl up to the higher levels of the underground lair, but the sheer number of goblins they had to slay along the way, as well as those still coming at them, was beginning to take a toll.

"We're almost there," hollered Mardra, perfectly calm

and in control of the situation. She was still the same girl Byron had met and fallen in love with back in Rosecrown. "It's only two more levels…"

"What's that?" asked Byron, feeling a quake beneath his feet.

"Not good," said Mardra.

Both the ground and the stone ceiling above began trembling, sending little shards of stone falling over their heads. The goblins, upon noticing this, gave up the fight and scattered, screeching and wailing in their goblin tongue.

"I can only imagine the mountain is crumbling," said Mardra. "Surely a trap set in place by Azar just in case. Make like these goblin cowards and run!"

Fear of being crushed under the mountain set their legs into spastic strides, and up each staircase Mardra went they followed, still hacking off the heads and arms of a few goblins here and there just for fun. The only obstacle now was jumping over and dodging the goblins that had tripped and fallen in their attempt at escape.

"We're almost at the last staircase!" cried Mardra.

As the gang followed along they were all thrown to the side and knocked over as the entire mountain shifted. Leigh and Lynette both fell backward down the staircase, luckily finding nets in the hands of Byron and Oberyl. Each twin was tossed back upward and onto their feet, and continued on dashing.

Light showed itself at the top of the staircase, but gradually decreased the nearer they came.

"The doorway is getting blocked by fallen rocks!"

shouted Mardra. "Hurry!"

By the time they reached the opening in the mountain, it had been completely sealed off by rubble.

"Shit!" cried Mardra as the rocky debris continued to fall on them, sending dust into their eyes.

"Byron," said Oberyl. "This is the only time I'm ever going to let you do this. So you had better enjoy it."

"Somehow, Oberyl chum, I think I know exactly what you're referring to." Byron looked over to Mardra and the twins. "Girls, stand aside. We're gonna need some room."

Byron grabbed Oberyl by the hands, and minding the limited space he had, very carefully began twirling his little friend around in a circle.

"Oh dear," cried one of the twins. "Will he be all right."

"Oh I'll be just fine, dear!" howled Oberyl as Byron's spins got faster and faster.

As Byron nearly reached the spinning speed of a cyclone he released Oberyl and sent the bulky little man whizzing through the air and into the rubble-barricaded exit.

"Cover your eyes and run straight!" cried Byron as a massive cloud of dust went flying their way.

Light returned to the cave as Oberyl's body busted through the rocks, and the gang scurried to it.

Mardra and the twins were impressed as they crossed over to the outside to find Oberyl standing up dusting himself off as if nothing had happened.

"Say Byron," began Oberyl, between spitting some dust out of his mouth. "Why would Parryn have needed a spell to get into the mountain, when there was just an entrance right there?"

"Good question," said Byron. "But there are more pressing matters at hand." Byron turned to Mardra and took in her voluptuous nude form.

"Agreed," said Oberyl, smiling and winking at Leigh and Lynette. "You girls are mighty fine warriors, I must say. I don't believe we've been properly introduced. I am Oberyl O'Garyn of—"

"Save it," said Mardra. "Just because we're out of the mountain doesn't mean it won't still crumble down on top of us."

"Good point," said Byron, and the five of them took off running down the path, dodging and hurdling falling boulders.

In a surprisingly short time they found themselves near the entrance to the path, marked by the overhanging dead tree branches.

"We've made it!" cried Byron, and instantly skidded on his heels coming to a dead stop. "Shit."

"Shit is right," grumbled Oberyl.

Before the five of them, spanning across the horizon for as far as they could see on either side, were warriors on horses.

"Say, Oberyl," began Byron, "the crests on their armor… Looks kind of familiar, doesn't it?"

"Indeed," said Oberyl.

"King Rainum's army from Zorathustin," said Mardra. "I take it they aren't reinforcements. Make a few enemies while you were away, love?"

"We might have, say, maybe pissed off a few people," Byron admitted.

"I think what he means to say, and by the way it is an honor and privilege to finally meet you, Mardra, is that *he* might have maybe killed both King Rainum and his queen."

"Good for you, Byron!" giggled Mardra. "I met them a couple times during my brief stint as queen of Rosecrown. They were dreadful company. Especially that Arianna. What a cunt."

"Agreed," said Byron. "Anyways, I wonder if we should surrender or run or something else along those lines."

From behind the frontline of riders from Zorathustin came what Byron and Oberyl hoped was a reassuring sight. Dressed in the garb of a queen with a gold crown upon her head, Lillia rode out to meet them brandishing a mighty broadsword. Behind her, also on horseback, came the hooded man and Parryn atop the same horse. They took the fact that Parryn was once again dressed and smiling to be a pretty good sign of things to come.

"Lillia," said Oberyl as the horses approached. "What pleasant surprise, I think."

"I would only hope so," said Lillia, and jumped down from her horse to give Oberyl a kiss. She sheathed her sword and said, "Turns out the hooded man was right. I did have my own part to play in all of this. Only it looks as if we showed up a bit too late to slay the goblin army."

"They won't be much of a problem," said Byron. "Unless they somehow survive that." Byron pointed back to the collapsing mountain, which as if on cue vanished with a massive, earth shaking boom and a giant cloud of dust.

"Well, it's good to see you've escaped with your lives," said Lillia, whose voice had rather quickly taken on a regal and queenly tone. "Now I believe someone would like to say hello to you, Byron."

The hooded man jumped down from his horse and approached Byron. In his hand was a burlap sack which dripped blood at the bottom.

"You helped me accomplish something I came back from the grave to do, Byron," said the hooded man, then reached into the sack and pulled out the head of Azar. "Thank you, old friend."

"For the love of the nine gods, Aldrick!" cried Byron. "Like we haven't known it was you the whole time! Just take your goddamn hood off already!"

Aldrick sighed in disappointment and threw back his hood, only to reveal the face of a much younger man than the one Byron had last seen.

"Aldrick," gasped Byron. "You look…about a thousand years younger. How'd you pull that one off?"

"Well, Byron, the nine gods are a funny bunch, I tell you. I guess when they get so fed up with a wizard in their netherworld and send him back to keep you from fucking up like you so often do, they throw in a few added perks."

"You were, or *are*, I should say, a rather dashingly handsome man in your youth," said Byron.

"Oh save it, you fuck," laughed Aldrick. "We've got plenty of time for flattery on the ride back to Zorathustin. They're going to have another party for you and Oberyl there. I think this one will go better than the last one."

"Let's hope," said Oberyl. "Let's really fucking hope."

Parryn dismounted and came up behind Aldrick, wrapping her arm around him.

"Parryn," said Byron. "Glad to see you made it out alive and unscathed."

"As am I," said Parryn.

"Not that's it's important anymore," began Byron, "but Oberyl here brought up a good point not long ago. Why did we need to find you and bring you along to recite a spell to get us into the mountain, when we just came out through an exit not too much farther down from where we got sucked in?"

"Why don't you explain that one, Aldrick my dear," said Parryn.

"The reason for that, Byron, is… Okay, look. There was never really a key, or spell, or whatever, that would get you into the mountain. That was just some bullshit I made up years ago. This is news to Parryn too. Let's just say I've always had the gift of foresight, more so than your average wizard or seer or mystic or whatever the fuck. I've been chasing Parryn here for years. I was never successful in winning her heart, seeing as the one thing my magic could never do was make me not look like a gross, saggy, crusty old man. I figured you two would never stop to pick someone up merely for assistance, seeing what a hurry you were in. So, by making you think you needed her just to gain entry, I kind of got everyone where I needed them to be at the same time, so I could help you save the continent from evil and doom and all that other shit, and win the heart of the girl I've been chasing for longer than any man should admit he's been chasing the same woman for. So I owe it all to you folks, and the nine gods for restoring my angelic looks of yore."

"So wait," scoffed Byron. "You knew all this shit was gonna happen, even before you died? And you never told me?"

"Remember what I said to you when I came to you in your dreams, Byron," laughed Aldrick. "The gods are the writers, and all that other philosophical bullshit. Who cares?" Aldrick turned to Queen Lillia's horsemen, then back to Byron and company. "Let's go get shitfaced!"

FIVE

The celebration, as all had hoped, went much better than the last one. Everyone was there. Leigh and Lynette found a happy place as heads of the guard in Queen Lillia's castle. Lillia had changed her mind about a life in royalty, as now she was able to live it on her own terms.

Aldrick was happy to settle down in his new life as the castle's healer, along with his partner mage Parryn, who seemed happy to leave her life as a bartender and whoremaster behind in Bahrmont.

Phadriel and the Sisters of Wisdom, along with the mighty dragon Mistria were in attendance too, though their arrival on Mistria's back set all in attendance into a fearsome moment of panic that nearly turned the whole party into a bloodbath. Oberyl was a little torn on matters of the heart when Phadriel first approached him, but much like Mardra, Lillia was the easygoing, understanding type. The three of them had disappeared for a time during the celebration.

Even Teela and the Centaurs showed up. Their arrival was only slightly less shocking to the people of Zorathustin than the arrival of the Sisters.

Byron and Mardra, however, were seldom seen throughout the majority of the party. Though, it was no great mystery to anybody where they were and what they were doing. Their privacy was respected.

As the celebration was winding down, King Oberyl strutted out onto the moonlit terrace where Byron stared out at the river. Just days ago the two had been in the exact same spot, under very different circumstances.

Byron turned to look down at Oberyl and laughed.

"I have to admit I was afraid that crown was going to be too big on you."

"Making fun of the king," said Oberyl. "I do believe that's an offense punishable by death. You're a mighty brave one, barbarian."

"Not even one day on the job and you're already a mad tyrant. The poor people of Zorathustin."

"Oh, I'll be the fairest and most just king there ever was," said Oberyl with a sigh. "Probably because I never really wanted to be a king. I merely accepted the position because, well, a lass like Lillia doesn't come around very often. And she's rich. And I'll be sleeping in a nice comfy bed every night for, well, probably the rest of my life. And I'll never have to pay for an ale or a good bag of pipe lea again. The only shitty part, barbarian, is that I owe it all to you." Oberyl paused to laugh. "That night I met you and Phadriel at that divey shit-hole in Peacebrook, if you had told me then that that chance meeting would result in this crown on my bald head, I'd have laughed in your face."

"I imagine you would have, had you a nice pair of stilts."

Oberyl punched Byron in the ribs and laughed again.

"Not many kings would let even their best friends talk to them like this."

"Not many kings are under five feet tall." Byron snickered for a moment grew serious. "You know, Oberyl, from here I think I can see the Forest of Torianne."

"Here we go with that sentimental bullshit again," laughed Oberyl.

"Oh, let me have my moment, will you?" said Byron. "It'll be some time until you're able to hear me lament like this again."

"So am I to take that as meaning you're turning down my offer?"

"Me? Byron the Barbarian, the hand of the king?" Byron looked up at laughed to the heavens. "The fact that I'll even refer to you, Oberyl O'Garyn of the Eerie, as my king should be more than enough. But what about you? You sure you're ready to rule a kingdom?"

"I think I told you this before, the last time you and I stood out on this terrace gazing out at the river, but I'll say it again. There was a time when I was a young fool just like you, Byron. How old are you, anyways?"

"Twenty," replied Byron.

"Yes, twenty," said Oberyl. "You must understand that that age was fifty-eight years ago for me. And back then I would have done just as you have done, and refused offers of nobility and kingship. I can understand why you wouldn't want to let *me* be your boss, as I've played the role of your sidekick. But after meeting Mardra, I think you were a damn fool to ever have left her side, especially with the offer of a crown. But I'll always think you're a damn fool, my friend. But, all that being said, I understand. Sixty years is a long time to be a travelling warrior. Even for one with the unnatural gift of prolonged life and slow aging."

"You never did tell me how you came to have that strange gift," said Byron.

"It's a tale for another tome," said Oberyl. "I imagine I'll be looking upon some downtime during this reign. That is, when I'm not ravaging my queen and her serving girls. And Phadriel will be making plenty of visits too. Yes, I asked Lillia, and she's not the jealous type."

"You savage beast!" hooted Byron.

"Anyhow, I'll probably take to chronicling the events of my life," said Oberyl. "Apparently kings are supposed to do that, according to Lillia. I do believe this king will have more interesting tales to write than the boring succession of noble brats who preceded me."

"When you came out here I had a feeling that this conversation was going to be about *me*," laughed Byron.

"Your tale has hardly just begun, friend," said Oberyl. "When you leave this castle, I'll expect you to return someday. Then I will want to hear all about *you*."

"You'll need that kind of entertainment, because I think you're going to get bored, friend," said Byron. "And you'll be missing both me and the sport of combat ever so dearly."

"You may be right," said Oberyl. "So make me a promise, will you?"

"For you, anything."

"You and Mardra come back here some day. I mean that. And after you tell me all your tales of grand adventure, this old king will sneak out and take to the high roads and low canyons again, even perhaps just once. But take your time, for I'm going to consider this whole ruling a kingdom thing a nice long vacation from swinging a hammer and sleeping in whorehouses. I suppose that's the part I'll miss most."

"I'd say we can call that a deal," said Byron, smiling down at his friend.

"That continent out there may be your home, Byron," said Oberyl, looking up at his hulking friend. "But this will always be your castle."

"Oberyl, I could just hug you right now."

"I would return that hug, but my face would be far too close to your cock. So, no offense, but how about a pat on the arse instead?"

"Shall we return to the party?" asked Byron, turning to find Mardra and Queen Lillia standing at the entrance between the terrace and the royal hall, decked out in tight white dresses that revealed much of their ample cleavage.

"Are you thinking what I'm thinking, Byron?" asked King Oberyl.

"Not a fucking chance," laughed Byron. "After what I went through to get her back, she's mine and mine only."

"You selfish fuck!" howled Oberyl as Byron walked away toward Mardra. "I helped, you know!"

EPILOGUE: THE GOLDEN SHOWER OF YOUTH

Travelling the continent and beyond with Mardra had been every bit the joy Byron imagined it would be. They sought treasures. They slayed monsters and made love on the corpse strewn battlefields, just as Byron had fantasized about since they first met. They explored the uncharted parts of the continent said to be rich in haunting and legendry. And sometimes, they pursued their own joys separately.

They had sailed, much to Byron's chagrin, off continent to the desert land of Virishka, where Mardra had wanted to visit the legendary spas for grooming, massage and beauty treatment. Byron, as a barbarian always does, had taken to the nearest watering hole in hopes of finding trouble.

Byron glanced around the smoky tavern. He loved everything about the place. The clouds that rose up from the many pipes and broadleafs added ambiance to the scene, making the sultry belly dancers drifting around the room look as though they were appearing to the barbarian in a dream.

The dancers' hips gyrated to the rhythmic drums and lutes that were being played by the band in the corner. Byron felt that this was a place he could retire to someday, if only he'd find a treasure grand enough to afford him such a thing as retirement from his business of axe swinging. Of course, Byron laughed at the idea no sooner that he thought it. He'd been made such offers twice in the past year, and refused them both.

One of the dancers in particular caught Byron's eye: a pale skinned girl with hair of gold. She was a vast departure from the other dancers who were copper of skin and had hair of flowing ebony.

A serving wench approached the lone barbarian asking, "Can I get you another ale?"

Byron nodded his answer, barely lifting an eye to the girl, nonchalantly keeping his focus on the blonde dancer. "Why not bring me two, girl?" he added. "Save yourself another trip. But don't worry. Your tip will still reflect the fine work you do."

"Right away, sir," said the girl, and hurried away to retrieve his drinks.

Lost was Byron in the serenity of his favorite dancer, his eyes watching her fluid movement around the tavern. Every man she passed whistled and in return was blown a kiss from her soft pink lips.

Among the many tables full of drunks and miscreants that she passed, there was one table occupied by a rather curious bunch which captured Byron's attention. At the head of the table sat a man wearing a turban made of fine purple cloth and adorned by a gleaming ruby right in the front center. The other men at the table, clearly underlings of the rich man, were dressed in the clothing of much poorer men; their faces were those of thieves and killers. Their discussion was hushed, but by reading their scarred, grizzly faces and watching their body language closely, Byron knew exactly what they were up to. Though he could not hear their words, there was no doubt they were speaking in the tongue of conspiracy.

Byron did his best to play it cool. Still hardly veteran of his trade, he practiced the art of listening without watching, and the tavern offered plenty of sights to behold while his ears focused elsewhere. Pleasantly he admired the graceful moves of the dancing girls with one eye, and enjoyed the tones that emanated from the small band of minstrels in the far corner with one ear. He guessed he needed more practice, though, for in the minutes that passed it appeared that he may have blown his cover, only not to the rich man in the fancy turban and his conspirators. The light-skinned dancer with the blonde hair locked eyes with him on several occasions.

Maybe she just likes me, thought Byron. I'm a new face here, a stranger among these parts. And for that very reason she may take me for a fool with coin ripe for the stealing. He suddenly realized his ears had lost their focus and joined his eyes in watching this girl closely like he had been before. Quickly he snapped himself out of his tunnel vision and sent his mind back to the table. Whatever the girl's reason could be for casting him such deliberate glances, he thought it best to keep a cautious eye on her.

For minutes Byron sat in awkward discomfort until he realized that the serving wench had yet to return with his drinks. *I suppose I'll just head over to the bar and fetch them myself.*

Byron got up and made his way through the dancers and the many patrons coming and going to the bar from their tables, also making a point to casually stroll by the table of the man in the turban. As he stepped by he picked up pieces of their conversation. Among the tidbits that he picked up he heard the man say something about a golden shower of youth. Suddenly it all made sense. Byron had heard of this very scheme a thousand times before. A man of wealth and nobility seeks a treasure. He comes to the one place where he's guaranteed to find ruthless, hungry men eager to do anything for the right price, and hires them for the job.

The golden shower of youth, thought Byron. Imagine that. I could stay young and virile forever, like Oberyl. And so could Mardra!

As casually as he possibly could, he glanced down at the table. There he saw a map of the town with a dotted line leading from one point to another. Drawn at the end of one line was a mountain. On the other end of the line was a cup, the map symbol for a tavern.

Byron knew he had lingered close to the table for too long when one of the grizzly men cast him a scornful glance and said, "Can we help you, sir?"

"I apologize for the intrusion, boys," replied Byron. "I'm new to these parts and it looked to me as though you were playing a game of stones, and I was merely hoping to join in.

I beg you all a thousand pardons, as I see I was mistaken."

"Fuck off then," said the man in the turban.

"Of course," replied Byron, and turned to the bar.

He took no more than two steps before he clumsily walked into someone, bumping chests. He had seen bloodshed on more than one occasion because of such clumsiness, but as the obstruction came clear before his eyes, his tension eased. In front of him stood the blonde dancer. She said nothing, only caressed his arms and shook her body to the beat of the minstrels. Gently she tugged on his arms, politely urging him to come with her. Not without keeping his guard up he followed. The girl continued pulling him along for much longer than he had expected, until the two were in a dark corridor in the back of the tavern where no eyes could see them.

"What is it you want from me?" asked Byron. "You've been watching me. Don't think I haven't noticed."

"I've noticed you watching me too, you fool," said the girl in a hushed whisper. "And all I'm trying to do is save your life."

"You save *my* life?" Byron laughed and pursed his lips. "And just from whom might you be saving me?"

"From that rich man and his table of thieves," said the girl. "If you used your ears half as well as your eyes you'd know."

"What do you mean, girl?"

"I mean that any fool with half their wits about them could see that you were listening to those men. Only you don't listen as well as you think. You don't really think I'm just some dancer, do you? I've been listening to them too. And while you were ogling me I must have heard them mention you at least ten times."

"Oh and what did they say?"

"Mostly they discussed the number of ways they were going to kill you, Byron."

"Wait…you know my name?"

"Of course I do, you fool," the girl replied. "And so do they. Your name is very well known among barbarians and treasure hunters."

"I see," said Byron. "Okay then, why are you trying to save my life, as you say?"

"I want more than just that. I want you to assist me."

"In what?"

"Doing exactly what those men are trying to do, only before they do it."

"Find the golden shower of youth?"

"Precisely," said the girl.

"And who are you?"

The girl began dancing to the music again and stepped away from Byron. "Beyond this corridor is the rear exit of the tavern. Go now to the Inn of the Cobra, and go quickly. The room with the half-moon painted on the door. I will meet you there. Kazarrat and his men will kill you if they see you again."

"Who?" asked Byron.

"Just go," the girl replied, and gracefully danced back into the tavern.

*

Byron waited patiently in the room with the half-moon painted on the door. He was surprised by just how nice the accommodations were, and found that the massive bed he sat upon might not be such a bad place to take a nap until the blonde girl should arrive.

What seemed like seconds later, Byron awoke to a gentle touch upon his forehead. On instinct he jerked and grabbed for his axe that was next to the bed, but eased his tension when he saw it was only the dancer.

"At ease, Byron," said the girl. "I'm glad you found my accommodations worthy. Are you rested?"

"I feel as though I've slept an entire night," replied Byron.

"You have indeed," said the girl, and opened the curtain to make way for bright beams of morning sunlight.

"That's impossible!"

"Not so. I thought many times to wake you, but I thought to sleep as well. It was quite comfortable lying there next to you. Why, I haven't shared a bed with a man since…oh it feels like centuries."

"We…" Byron's question trailed off to silence.

"No, you fool," laughed the girl. "I held you close and we snored the night away."

"I see," said Byron, sighing in relief.

"Now tell me," began the girl. "What do you know of the so-called golden shower of youth?"

"Legend tells that it hides in the depths of a cave, not far from these lands," said Byron. "Legend also claims it is guarded by the goddess Lila, the goddess of youth. And should you drink from its waters you return to a state of youthfulness and remain that way forever."

"Close enough to what I've heard," said the girl.

"Now, it is time for you to tell me just who you are," said Byron. "I've been far too trusting of a complete stranger thus far. Especially one who works in disguise and has a keen ability to listen to strangers from afar."

"Again, Byron, who I am is of no importance. I'm merely a girl whose people hold the golden shower of youth as something sacred. What is important is who that man in the purple turban is, and that we stop him from finding the fountain."

"I've no doubt I can stop this man, as well as take him and his four henchman down. But what help are you going to be to me in doing so?"

"I know where the fountain is," replied the girl.

"And just how so?"

"I've been there."

*

Byron and the girl set out on camelback after a quick breakfast at the inn, and found themselves at the cave within two turns of an hourglass.

Byron was disappointed.

"This is it?" he asked.

"What had you expected?" replied the girl.

"Something a little grander than a simple hole in a mountain. We're talking about a fountain of legend, supposedly guarded by a deity. Speaking of which, if this fountain is divinely protected, what need is there for us to save it. This Lila, goddess of youth, can't do it herself?"

"Do not speak ill of the gods, barbarian. There are more to these things than you know."

"And what do you know of gods, girl?"

"No more than the average man or woman. Now come on. Light our torches and let's move."

Byron reached for the torches that were strapped to his camel, but let out a thundering curse as something blunt struck his head and left a sting.

"Take cover!" cried the girl.

Byron, not being one to run and hide so easily, turned in the direction from which the object had been flung. There, standing on a ridge just above the cave's entrance was the purple-turbaned man and his four henchman.

"Kazarrat!" the girl cried.

"You two are a little late," said Kazarrat. "And we heard you coming loud and clear."

"Well then," began Byron, "why not come down here and try taking my head off with your own blade instead of tossing rocks like a child."

Byron was answered by yet another hurled rock from a henchmen's slingshot, followed by a rapid succession of others.

"I can dodge rocks all day," said Byron. "Unless you can conjure up a bit of magic, this day will be your last."

Kazarrat made a wave of his hand and uttered what sounded like gibberish, but was more like what Byron feared, a spell of dark magic spoken in an ancient forbidden tongue.

The pile of rocks that sat before Byron and the girl began trembling and coalescing into one form.

"Ask and you shall receive, Byron," laughed Kazarrat as he and his men jumped down from the ridge and darted into the cave.

*

Sparks spat through the air as steel clanged against rock. Kazarrat's magic was indeed of the darker breed, proven by the massive humanoid creature that was only moments ago a pile of rocks.

Byron was hardly surprised by the monster. In his years he had done battle with dirt dwellers, murdlochs, and sea monsters, just to name a few. What did take him by surprise, however, was the adeptness with which the girl assisted him in combat. From seemingly out of nowhere she had produced a scimitar blade that she wielded with expert precision.

Her assistance seemed to do little, though, toward drawing them nearer to the end of this little battle.

"How long are we going to stand here hammering away like this?" cried Byron in between slices of his blade.

"You go on into the cave, Byron!" replied the girl. "Let me worry about this monster!"

"Are you mad?" laughed Byron before dodging the swing of a mighty rock-hand. "We'll see this through together!"

The girl, insulted, leaped high, and with a forceful thrust swung her blade into the crevice where two boulders formed the creature's neck joint. Chips of rock flew in all directions as she pulled her blade back, and the monster's head tilted far to the left. This had put a stagger into the creature's step, and the girl laughed at Byron with satisfaction.

"You've proven your point, girl," said Byron. "But I'll still not leave you to battle this monster on your own."

"Fine!" the girl cried, and leapt high again, this time taking the creature's head completely off. "Arrogant man," she added as the rock-monster crumbled back into a pile of stones. "Come on now. You light the torches and follow me. They couldn't have gotten far."

*

Byron was making quick work of two of Kazarrat's men while the girl displayed the same adeptness in combat as she had shown against the rock-monster.

Kazarrat and his band of mercenaries had gotten farther than the girl had thought they would, and Kazarrat was nowhere in sight, but there was no question as to whether or not he had located the fountain.

The sound of pouring, streaming water could be heard from beyond an entrance to a smaller cave within the cave. And between clangs and slashes the sound of deep, maniacal laughter echoed from out of the small room.

"It's too late, girl!" cried Byron.

"It's never as late as you think!" the girl called back between slices of her sword. "We must make quick work of these four and you'll see just what I mean."

Again Byron had the feeling that he was somehow being led on or deceived by the girl.

Suddenly, an unexpected sound replaced Kazarrat's deep laughter, and the swordplay instantly ceased.

"Is that what I think it is?" Byron asked the girl.

"Indeed, barbarian," she replied with a laugh.

Kazarrat's henchmen exchanged confused glances. They knew perfectly well what was going on; the confusion was merely an unresolved question of what they should do next. Predictably, the four of them turned tail and ran, shouting curses and grunts as they fled to find their next job.

"Follow me," said the girl, and turned to walk through the small doorway that led to the fountain.

Cautiously, Byron followed with axe still drawn.

Before him he saw perhaps the most exotically beautiful sight he'd ever seen, marred by a rather horrific sight. Surrounded by a rim of solid gold was the clearest, purest water he'd ever laid eyes upon. Intricate stone statues adorned the cavern walls. The barbarian stood in awe, feasting his eyes on the wonder that was the golden shower of youth. However, floating in midair above the water was a massive humanoid with the face of an elephant. From the crotch of the creature hung a giant gray phallus that was pissing all over what appeared to be a pile of clothing.

"Pay attention, barbarian," said the girl, and pointed down to the rim of the water.

Byron had been so lost in the cavern's beauty and the ghastly elephant cock, he had forgotten the strange noise that brought the fight to an abrupt halt. Snapping back to reality he heard it once again: over the sounds of streaming elephant piss was the howling and crying of a newborn infant.

The pile of clothing was the purple robes of Kazarrat, with his turban sitting atop them. The girl knelt down and removed the turban from the pile, revealing a perfectly innocent infant underneath it.

"The golden shower of youth," laughed Byron. "It's all a joke, isn't it? And somehow I think you've known all along, girl."

"My fountain is no joke," said the girl as she stood cradling the infant body of Kazarrat. "It is the sacred place of rebirth for the deities of these people. And arrogant treasure hunters who bother not to learn the original languages of men, the languages in which the texts of my religion have been translated from countless times, find out the hard way that a few important things about the fountain aren't quite as clear as they are in the old texts. If you drink from the fountain, your youth is indeed restored, as you can see by the child in my arms. But if you are not a deity, you start life over in a realm of the nine hells."

"Hold on," said Byron. "Your fountain? You just called this *your* fountain. Is that your pissing elephant too?"

"I had hoped you'd figure it out on your own, barbarian," laughed the girl. She turned and pointed to the largest statue in the cavern. Byron gasped as he saw it was an exact replica of her own image.

"You?" asked Byron. "Lila? The Goddess of Youth? Why didn't you tell me? All this time, you were a goddess. I risked my life fighting monsters and henchman of that baby in your arms, and you never needed me."

"I was testing you, Byron. It is what deities do. I thank you." Lila began walking toward Byron, looking deep into his eyes. "Now for your reward."

Lila reached her face up to Byron and placed her lips softly against his, giving him a deep but gentle kiss.

"Did you just grant me eternal youth?" asked Byron.

"No, you idiot," replied Lila with a laugh. "But the kiss of a goddess has been known to offer mortal men some much needed help in desperate times. I know what perils you are to face next. You might need it. Farewell, Byron."

Byron stood in awed silence as Lila carried the infant Kazarrat toward her very own statue and vanished in a flash of light.

"If you know what perils I am to face next, why not tell me?" Byron asked the statue.

"Perhaps answering to your lover for sleeping the night away with a dancing girl," came the voice of Mardra from the entrance to the sacred cave. "And for forgetting to meet your lover at the spa when she was through with her hot bath and nail treatment."

Byron was lost for words.

"Nothing to say, my barbarian lover?" asked Mardra.

"You followed me here?"

"Yes, Byron."

"You saw me fight that rock monster and didn't even

help?"

"I saw you and your little dancing girl fight the rock monster," scoffed Mardra. "And why help? *She* seemed to have the situation perfectly under control. Typical of you."

"I… I was going to come find you," gasped Byron, shaking off the sting of Mardra's insult. "I had no interest in the girl, I swear. I was just… Just ask the elephant! You'll see!"

Byron turned to the sacred elephant that stood above the fountain. The humanoid deity had, much like Lila, disappeared into its statue.

"I've every desire to shove you into that fountain and let that elephant piss all over you so I can raise you into a thoughtful barbarian instead of a dimwit. But, this is the price I pay for loving a barbarian."

Mardra came over to Byron and gently punched him in the gut, then stood up on the tips of her toes to kiss him softly on the lips.

"Is all forgiven, my dear?" asked Byron.

"I suppose so," laughed Mardra. "Now come along. While I was at the spa I overheard some talk of treasure hidden in a graveyard not far from here."

Jeff O'Brien writes and edits books. He lives in southern New Hampshire with his wife and their four dogs: Chewie, Velma, Scully and Falcor.

BYRON
the Barbarian
Book One: The Sorceress Queen
JEFF O'BRIEN

SEQUEL TO THE SORCERESS QUEEN
BYRON
the Barbarian
Book Two:
The Horror of Castle Valgorn
JEFF O'BRIEN

JEFF O'BRIEN'S
BIGBOOBENSTEIN

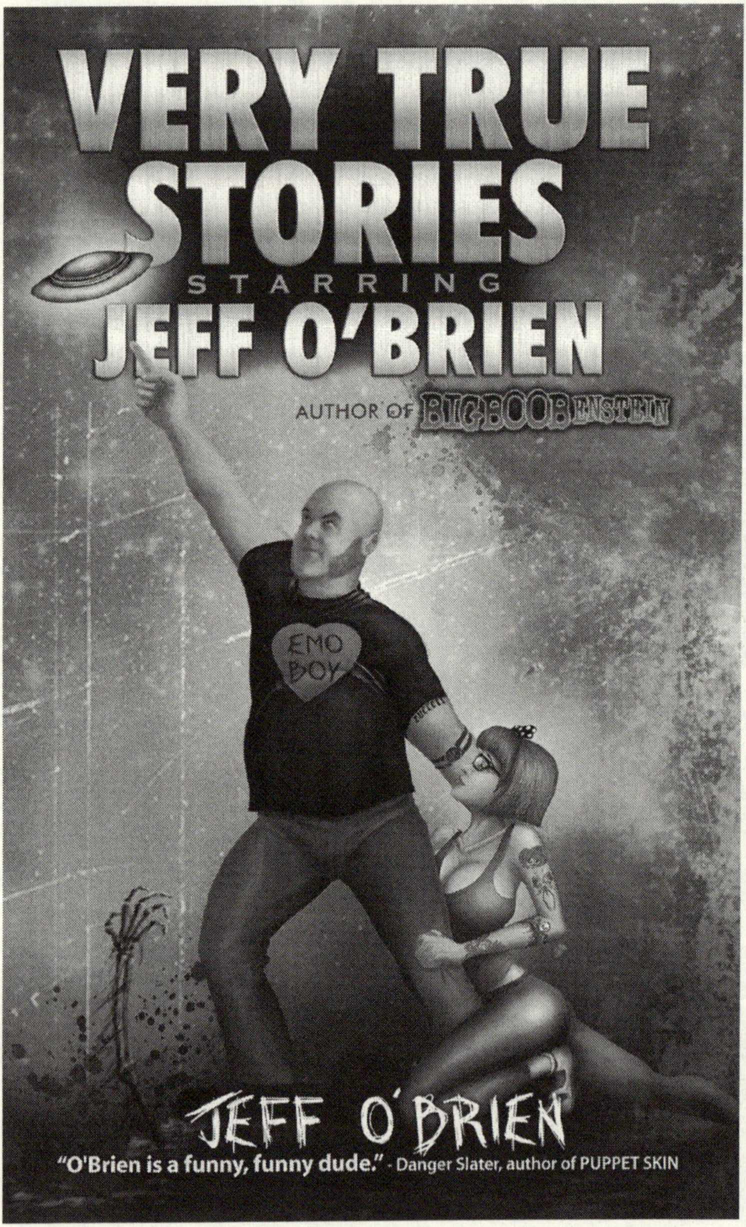
VERY TRUE STORIES
STARRING
JEFF O'BRIEN
AUTHOR OF BIGBOOBENSTEIN
EMO BOY
JEFF O'BRIEN
"O'Brien is a funny, funny dude." - Danger Slater, author of PUPPET SKIN

HEART-SHAVED
BOX
HOLY BIBLE
JEFF O'BRIEN
AUTHOR OF BIGBOOBENSTEIN

Support indie authors.
Write a review.

61854574R00083

Made in the USA
Lexington, KY
22 March 2017